Blackberry Pie

By Bonnie Dee

A young minister's celibacy is challenged by an earthy, Appalachian woman.

On a blistering summer afternoon, Reverend Nathan Andrews climbs a mountain to meet backwoods members of his congregation. Fresh from seminary, the young man isn't prepared for the onslaught of lust that hits him when he encounters a sensuous girl picking blackberries.

Determined to implement his outreach plan, he helps her harvest the fruit. But their potent sexual chemistry is too intense to deny and they engage in passionate sex surrounded by the beauty of nature.

Grace is earthy and primal, the opposite of the proper young lady he expects to take as a wife some day. Can there possibly be a future for a college-educated minister and a primitive mountain girl?

Warning, this title contains the following: explicit sex, graphic language.

D1520033

Liaisons in Jubilee
By Jamie Craig

Sometimes the truth is the greatest aphrodisiac.

Katie Mayes is the Executive Manager for a large, east coast beach resort. Unfortunately, her boss has discovered her one secret – her seasonal flings with Caleb Beckett, the Entertainment Director for the resort. Company policy dictates no internal fraternization, especially between managers and their subordinates, so her boss gives Katie a choice. Caleb or her job.

She avoids personal encounters with Caleb, until one fateful night a week before the resort's big summer launch. Then, she runs into him at a local nightclub. When Caleb approaches her, she tries to give him the cold shoulder, but he follows her onto the dance floor where the music, her desire, and his persistence break her will. She claims it's only one more night before they break it off completely, but Caleb insists on more. Far from an ending, he views the summer as their true beginning.

Warning, this title contains the following: explicit sex, graphic language, spanking, light bondage.

Second Wind

By Dee S. Knight

Cocky cowboy Rafe Walker doesn't plan to meet a beautiful woman in designer jeans and ostrich skin boots at the rodeo, but the beauty catches his gaze just before the gate opens for his bull ride. Talk about losing focus! With one glance, his thoughts are of sex-scented sheets, not hard, dirt.

A city girl like her would never fit in on his ranch, but a weekend in Dallas? Yes, Ma'am, she'll do just fine. Little does he expect a ride wilder than with any bull. She grabs hold of his heart and his hottest fantasies and holds on tight.

Cathy Fitzgerald, raised in a wealthy eastern family, half falls in love with the rakish cowboy after one impulsive weekend of wild sex. She returns to Boston, breaks off her near engagement and waits to hear from Rafe. After months of silence, he surprises Cathy with a proposal. It's a shock to both of them when she accepts, and moves to his ranch in nowhere, Texas.

They soon find that passion alone can't sustain a marriage. Rafe's pride and Cathy's long hours at work breed distrust and broken hearts. Giving their marriage its second wind will take an act of nature.

Warning, this title contains the following: explicit sex and graphic language.

Hunk of Burnin' Love
By Veronica Wilde

Falling in lust with a sexy Elvis impersonator gets complicated when Vanessa discovers the real Elvis Presley may have hoaxed his death.

Summer should mean hot men and toe-curling sex—at least that's what Vanessa believes, but a bad break-up has left her spending her summer nights alone. Then her sex life erupts into flames when she meets two very different Elvis impersonators on the same night. One is a sexy young musician who gets her all shook up in a steamy midnight swim. The other is a graying older man who looks just a little too much like Elvis Presley for comfort.

Vanessa can't help falling in love with her new summer hottie. But their burning love gets complicated when the mysterious older impersonator begins dropping disturbing hints about his true identity—hints that suggest Elvis Presley never died at all.

Warning, this title contains the following: explicit sex and graphic language.

Heat Wave

A Samhain Publishing, Ltd. publication.

Samhain Publishing, Ltd.
577 Mulberry Street, Suite 1520
Macon, GA 31201
www.samhainpublishing.com

Heat Wave
Print ISBN: 978-1-59998-777-4
Blackberry Pie Copyright © 2008 by Bonnie Dee
Liaisons in Jubilee Copyright © 2008 by Jamie Craig
Second Wind Copyright © 2008 by Dee S. Knight
Hunk of Burnin' Love Copyright © 2008 by Veronica Wilde

Editing by Sasha Knight
Cover Art by Anne Cain

Blackberry Pie
First Samhain Publishing, Ltd. electronic publication: June 2007
Liaisons in Jubilee
First Samhain Publishing, Ltd. electronic publication: August 2007
Second Wind
First Samhain Publishing, Ltd. electronic publication: August 2007
Hunk of Burnin' Love
First Samhain Publishing, Ltd. electronic publication: July 2007
First Samhain Publishing, Ltd. print publication: May 2008

Contents

Blackberry Pie

Bonnie Dee

Dedication

Thanks to all friends and family who have been supportive of my writing obsession.

Chapter One

When he first glimpsed her out of the corner of his eye, he thought she was a forest animal, a deer foraging for food. If he looked at it directly, the wild creature would crash through the undergrowth and disappear into the emerald depths of the woods. His gaze swung toward the movement in the briar patch and focused, but she didn't run.

A pair of deep brown doe eyes stared back at him. The animal frozen among the brambles was human. The sun shone on the crown of her dark brown hair, picking out strands of gold and red. The tangled, curly mane spilled around her thin face and down her back. Sweaty tendrils stuck to her forehead and fell across one eye.

Her eyes drew him back again. They dominated her small face so much that he scarcely noticed the elegant, high bridge of her nose or bowed upper lip of her mouth.

Nathan's gaze slipped from her eyes to her body. The girl wore a sleeveless dress of fabric so thin it clung to her like a second skin. The shift may once have been colorful, but was now so faded and threadbare it was a dingy off-white. But the cheap, cotton dress was merely a setting for a precious stone. The girl's slender arms, sharp collarbones and long neck were a warm tan against the pale fabric. Underneath the translucent material pressed the swell of her breasts and the small, hard shape of nipples.

Inside his sober black pants, so very hot from absorbing the sun's rays, Nathan's cock stiffened. Ashamed of his brazen perusal of her body and its effect on him, his gaze snapped back up to her face. The girl's wide eyes held a glitter of inherent awareness of his lustful thoughts, although perhaps it was only reflected sunlight.

The exchange transpired in moments, but felt like an eternity in which they were suspended like ants in amber.

Sweat trickled down Nathan's spine, itchy and tickling. The armpits of his shirt were wet and, after an hour of rambling through the wilderness, he wished he'd worn one with short sleeves. His black jacket was draped over one arm. He'd abandoned it after the first twenty minutes of hiking. His clerical collar was tucked in one of the jacket's pockets.

The open glade in the woods was somnolent with heat, the air so thick and muggy a person could drown in it. He hadn't known the mountains in summer would be so humid. Back at seminary he'd pictured the Blue Ridge much differently than it actually was—more Alps than Appalachia.

The amber moment had run its course. Nathan needed to speak before the silence grew any more awkward. He stretched the corners of his mouth up into a smile. "Hello." He half-expected the wild-looking girl to startle at the sound of his voice and bound off into the woods.

"How-do." She inclined her head as slowly and graciously as a queen accepting her subject's homage.

"I'm the new minister, Reverend Nathan Andrews." He moved a few steps toward her, but was confronted by a thicket of blackberry briars and had to stop. "I'm out today, hoping to meet some of the community." *The non-church-attending backwoods members of my congregation.*

"Mm." Her eyes scanned him up and down more leisurely and lingering than he had dared look at her. "Might hot for visitin', ain't it?"

His smile became more sincere. "Yes, it is. But I've found when it's not steaming hot here, it's pouring rain. This seemed slightly more agreeable weather."

The girl walked toward him, passing carefully through the briars without once snagging her clothes. She stopped when she stood only a few feet from him. "Ain't you young for a preacher?"

He could smell her hot skin, her ripe, feminine sweat, not unpleasant but natural and heady as catnip. Scratches marked her arms in thin, long streaks. A wooden bucket dangled from one of her hands. It was half-filled with deep purple berries. Nathan glanced down at her bare legs and feet under the hem of her dress. More scratches and dusty grime coated her high-arched feet and lean, brown legs.

Again he brought his attention back to her face. "I just graduated in spring. Class of '34. This is my first church."

She nodded, looked at his black coat and white shirt, which had been crisply ironed when he put it on that morning, then back to his face again. "I'm Grace."

"Pleased to meet you, Grace." He extended his hand to shake hers.

She stared at it a moment before taking it. Her slim hand was warm and damp with sweat. He supposed his was too. Her palm was hard with calluses, not soft and delicate as it appeared. Her fingers curled around his hand and released it slowly like vines clinging to a trellis. Nathan felt the ghostly

13

pressure of her hand even after it was gone. An electric tingling vibrated through his flesh.

"Blackberry?" She held up her bucket. The sweet aroma that had teased his senses since he entered the glade rose strong and potent from the mass of fruit.

"Thank you." He reached into the bucket and picked a berry. It was pulpy and moist from the heat. He nodded at the girl and popped the fruit into his mouth where it burst, syrupy and rich. Hard seeds crunched in contrast to the mushy flesh of the fruit.

She watched him chew. Her gleaming eyes made the act seem too intimate, as if he was doing something other than eating in front of her. Although the bite of berry was small, Nathan swallowed hard. "Very sweet. Thank you," he said again.

"This 'ere's the best patch around." The girl lifted a berry to her own mouth. Her indigo-stained tongue slipped out between rosy lips. She placed the berry on her tongue and drew it slowly back inside.

Nathan watched, mesmerized, searching for something to say, but his mind was completely blank. Pleasantries like asking about her family, where she lived, whether she ever attended the Grace Baptist Church—which ironically shared her name—all that was beyond him. He could only stare at her moving mouth and the subtle fluctuation in her throat as she swallowed. His erection swelled harder and he backed away a step, looking past Grace at the blackberry patch. "What will you make with the berries?"

"Preserves and pie." She reached into her bucket and selected another berry. Her eyes sparkled like the sun on a dark pool as she extended her hand toward his mouth. If chewing in front of her had felt intimate, the offering from her fingers directly to his lips was downright erotic. Her eyes challenged him to open his mouth and accept the fruit, and he couldn't refuse it without looking like a flustered fool.

He opened his mouth, throat dry as sandpaper, and felt the feather-light touch of her fingers brushing his lips and the berry settling on his tongue.

She smiled as she withdrew her hand and let it drop back to her side.

His heart pounded like a blacksmith's hammer. His cheeks blazed with heat and blood rushed in his ears. His cock throbbed in time to his rapid heartbeats. The glade's heat seemed intensified, smothering. Nathan's head swam and he wondered if he was about to pass out—all because a country girl hand-fed him a blackberry.

A charge like ionized air before a thunderstorm smoldered between them for several seconds before the girl broke it by speaking. "Must be thirsty from all the walkin'. There's a stream over yonder." She pointed toward the woods on the far side of the glade.

"Yes, water would be good," he agreed weakly.

"Best come 'round the patch lessen you want to get your nice clothes all ruined." She turned and walked in front of him, hips swaying slightly from side to side.

It took every ounce of Nathan's willpower to drag his gaze away from the undulations of her hips and buttocks and the long, lean legs stretching down below the short hem of her shift.

"You been to Cadey's Pass, seen the family up there yet?" she asked as she led him up a slope and through a stand of pine trees. He heard the trickling of water and his mouth salivated in response.

"Um, no. I had directions, but got lost on the way."

"Easy to get twisted 'round on the mountain." Her light voice drifted back over her shoulder, rising up and down with a musical lilt.

"Where do you live?" he finally remembered to ask. "What's your last name?"

"Owl Ridge over yonder. Last name's Parkins." She stopped walking suddenly and Nathan ran into her. He stepped back so quickly he tripped on a branch half-buried in the leaf mold. It took him a few stumbling steps to regain his balance.

"Here." She crouched and pushed back a tall clump of ferns to reveal water bubbling right up out of the ground and meandering away in a thin stream. "It's plenty cold." She lay down on her belly and bent her face to the surface of the water.

Nathan could hardly breath, watching her natural ease as she sprawled on the ground and scooped water to her mouth. Her dress rode even higher, revealing a lightly haired expanse of leg all the way up to the rounded shadow where her thighs met her bottom. He swallowed the hard lump in his throat and raised his eyes to the canopy of green leaves above them. This was a test—surely a test from God of Nathan's dedication to the ideal of chastity.

Back in the seminary it had been easy to talk analytically with his peers about moral and spiritual matters. The seminarians all expected to work in the mission field for a year or two, return home to meet and marry a suitable young woman and begin life as a family man. Full of religious fervor and the desire to grow new spiritual communities, none of them considered delaying sexual gratification a problem. The young men had been celibate so long, what was another year or two? But out in the world, Nathan had discovered working with real people was considerably more complicated than he'd anticipated, and today's sudden, unexpected and powerful surge of physical desire for a strange young woman took him completely by surprise.

"Ain't you thirsty?"

He looked down at Grace. She had pushed up off the ground and squatted by the water, looking up at him, her lips glistening wet. Her hair was darker here in the shadows with no sun highlighting it. Her eyes looked darker too. She gazed at him over one bare shoulder, the sleeve of her shift having slipped down her arm. The vulnerability of the soft curve of flesh made his heart twist. She looked like a young girl wearing her older sister's too-large dress.

"Yes," he finally answered her question.

He dropped to his knees on the leafy forest floor, setting his jacket aside. With one hand pressed flat to the ground, he lowered his face close to the bubbling stream and scooped icy cold handfuls of water to his mouth. The sharp mineral tang soothed his throat and cooled his raging libido a little—until he turned his head and faced Grace's eyes, only a couple of feet away, looking back into his.

She smiled and her eyes crinkled at the corners, her lashes making a long, lacy fringe around them. Her full lips parted to reveal a flash of white teeth then closed again, as she regarded him solemnly, her gaze lingering on his mouth. For one heart-stopping moment, Nathan thought she was going to lean in and kiss him, but she sat back on her heels, hands resting on her lap.

Nathan sat too, closing his eyes for a moment to gather his senses before he looked at her again. When he opened them, she was still there, not a fairytale sprite of the woods, but a flesh and blood young woman with dirty feet and berry-stained fingers.

"Don't get many visitors up here," she said. "How long you been preaching at the church?"

"Almost two months. It's taken me some time to get around to meeting the whole community. Families are spread out all over the mountain."

Grace laughed. "And half of 'em got some grudge or feud goin' on with the other half. You can't spit for fear of rilin' somebody." She shook her head. "Best to try an' keep out of it, but tain't enough for people to get mad at each other—they want everybody to choose up sides."

Nathan smiled, feeling easier as her talk filled the awkward silence. "It doesn't make my job easy, trying to convince people to 'turn the other cheek'."

Grace rose to her feet, extending a hand to him. He couldn't refuse to take it without appearing rude. She grasped his hand firmly and pulled him to his feet with more strength in her slim body than he would have guessed. She continued holding his hand and looking up at him.

Almost a head shorter than he, Grace made Nathan feel big and masculine, words he didn't usually associate with himself. His mind had been immersed in books and theology for so long, he'd forgotten what it was like to indulge in more sensual pursuits. Something as simple as holding a girl's hand or enjoying a sweet blackberry on a hot day took on an aspect of sinful pleasure.

"Well...thank you for the water. It was very refreshing. I suppose I'd better be going."

A flicker of something crossed her eyes, disappointment or maybe nothing but a shadow caused by a fluttering leaf overhead. "You could tarry a while." Her voice was low and soft. "Pick blackberries with me. Or, iffen you don't care to dirty your clothes, you could talk to me while I pick."

Nathan dragged his gaze away from her mesmerizing eyes, glanced up the mountain then back at her. "I should be getting on. I've a number of stops I intended to make today."

"Ain't I one of the folks you came up here to meet?" Releasing his hand, she raised an eyebrow and folded her arms beneath her breasts. The shape and color of her dark nipples pressed against the almost transparent, limp fabric.

He blinked and looked away. "I—I suppose you are at that." His quick, sharp smile was almost a grimace. He felt he was standing on a precipice and the edge was crumbling underneath his feet.

"I'll send some berries home with you. Who's keepin' house for you?"

"Um, Mrs. Crowder. She cooks and cleans."

"She can make you a cobbler." Allowing no further argument, Grace took his hand in hers and pulled him through the patch of woods to the clearing again.

Chapter Two

Out from under the shelter of trees, the heat trapped in the little hollow of weeds and blackberry brambles was oppressive. The sun bore down on the crown of Nathan's head like a heavy hand weighing on him. He pushed his hand through his sweaty, brown hair, lifting it from his scalp so the air could pass through it. He should've immersed his whole head in the spring water. That would've kept him cool for a while.

"Too hot? You can set under yonder tree if you'd care to."

"No. I'll help you pick." Nathan had decided the best way to gain trust as a minister was to show his flock he would work alongside them. A spiritual laborer shouldn't be too proud to physically labor with his congregation on occasion.

"Then best remove your shirt. Blackberry stains don't never come out."

Nathan hesitated, torn between the logic of her words and the inappropriateness of being half-garbed, alone with a woman. Finally he unbuttoned his shirt, shrugged it off and laid it with his jacket underneath a tree. Wearing only a sleeveless T-shirt, he felt instantly cooler—and conversely hotter. A brush of air touched his bare arms and neck, but so did Grace's eyes, sending hot licks of fire through him.

She handed him an empty bucket. "I done this patch over here. Y'might try just over there." She indicated where he should pick and Nathan obediently moved to the clump of bushes. The berries were clustered high on the canes, but Grace cautioned him to check beneath the leaves as well. "Ever picked blackberries afore?"

"No, but I harvested vegetables in my mother's garden and picked apples at my uncle's farm every fall."

"Where y'all from?"

"Michigan."

She nodded. "Yankee. Thought your talk was strange. How'd you come here?"

"I graduated from Princeton Theological Seminary and there were job postings for mountain churches in need of pastors. I'd never been south before. I wanted to see the mountains and minister to a congregation in need." He didn't tell her it was also because he'd been told the mission was a difficult outreach, the mountain people stubborn and resistant to change, and Nathan had wanted the challenge.

She moved closer to him, pulling aside a thorny branch and showing him ripe clusters he'd missed. "Y'all like it down here?"

"The mountains are beautiful, and the people have been...very welcoming."

She looked up at him with a skeptically raised eyebrow. "Doubtful you been up at Cadey's Pass or down in Possum Holler then."

He smiled. "All right, I'll admit some members of the community haven't appreciated a stranger in their midst. I'm sure, given time, they'll get used to me."

She laughed and copied his accent flawlessly. "Given twenty years or so perhaps." Resuming her southern twang, she added, "But I don't reckon you're plannin' on stayin' that long."

"I doubt it," he admitted.

For a short while silence fell between them as they moved through the berry patch under the hot August sun. Only a blackbird's musical trill and the whine of an occasional mosquito near Nathan's ear disturbed the quiet. His fingers were soon purple-tipped and his hands covered with scratches from the lethal thorns on the blackberry canes. No matter how careful he was, he kept brushing against them, snagging their barbs on his skin. The jagged scratches stung from his salty sweat.

Soon the bottom of Nathan's bucket was covered with several inches of fruit. He glanced at Grace, intent on her picking, and decided he should make an attempt at ministering since that was what he was here for after all. "So, Grace, does your family ever attend church? I haven't seen you there yet. I know it's quite a distance for you."

"Distance ain't the problem. Somethin' you gotta understand, preacher. The folks at the bottom of the mountain is one kind, but up here on the ridge we have our own way of doin' things. We don't tend toward church-goin' much. Leastways not me."

"Why not?" His hand rested on the rim of the tin pail as he watched her hands move briskly and efficiently over the canes, harvesting berries.

"Got my momma's Bible for readin' from, but I'd rather spend time with God out here on a Sunday"—she gestured up at the clear blue sky above them—"'stead of in a church buildin'."

"But you believe in God."

"Shore. How could a body look around and not?" She faced him, setting her bucket down at her feet then pushing her hair back behind her ears. "Look at all this. And you. And me." She gave him a smile that didn't quite reach her solemn eyes. "Reckon God had a hand in it."

Indeed, he thought, his breath stolen by the girl's beauty. Her tangled hair was a wild, dark halo around her head. Her eyes were shiny, obsidian pools, depthless and secretive. And her mouth...if he walked two steps closer and inclined his head, he could cover her lush lips with his. He fought against the powerful urge, shoving it down inside him.

Then suddenly the struggle was removed from his hands as Grace took the two steps toward him and laid her hand on his chest. He felt her warm touch through the thin cotton of his undershirt. She must be able to feel his chest rising and falling and his heart beating like a jackrabbit's hind foot.

She tilted her head, looking up into his eyes. "How can a world so full a life not have somethin' makin' it so?" She paused a moment as if honestly waiting for an answer. Her dark eyes were like a pair of burning coals searing him. They drifted shut as she rose up on her toes. One of her hands hooked around his neck pulling him down to her. Lips as soft as flower petals brushed his.

He gasped quietly in surprise, then his mouth closed over hers, responding instinctively to her kiss. Her mouth was wet, warm and yielding. His lips fed on hers, light presses that slowly became hungrier, more aggressive. The handle of the pail slipped from his fingers. Dimly he heard it hit the ground, as his hands stole up to cup her face and hold it steady. He angled his head to settle his mouth more firmly over hers.

Grace leaned into him, wrapping her arms around his neck and clinging to him. Her breasts pressed against his chest, soft, malleable mounds of flesh that sent waves of desire sweeping through him. His cock responded to her proximity, rising erect and hard between them.

It was wrong. He had to stop it before they went too far.

Every cell in his body was alive and vibrating with need. Heat radiated from his body and hers, melding them together into one incandescent being.

It was perfect, right and natural. How could he end such bliss?

"No!" Letting go of her mouth with a gasp, he pushed her away from him. "I'm sorry. I didn't mean to..."

"I did. I meant to." She gazed at him with eyes so dilated they appeared black, and shook her head. "Ain't nothing wrong with it. Just kissing. Didn't you like it?"

"Yes. Of course, but that's not the point. I—I'm a minister. I'm supposed to be..." What he was supposed to be? He'd forgotten. "Giving spiritual guidance."

"Don't need it." Slipping her hands around his waist, she moved in close again.

"I... We don't even know each other. We just met. It's not appropriate."

"Why not?" She had to tilt her head back to look up into his eyes.

"You're very young." He gripped her shoulders intending to push her away once more and yet he kept holding them. "Too young. I'd be taking advantage of you."

Her laughter tinkled like wind chimes on a breeze. "You're young too. Maybe I'd be the one takin' advantage. Think I'm an ignorant country girl, too dumb to know my own mind?"

"No." His hands slid from her shoulders down to her wrists to remove her hands from his waist, but paused there. "But 'just kissing' can lead to other things. It's immoral to indulge in bodily pleasures without the blessing of marriage."

Grace made a scoffing sound and pulled him even tighter to her. "You tellin' me you never messed around with a gal afore?"

Nathan's face burned at her bluntness. "Not like this." He thought of the times he'd walked Mary Albright home after Sunday school, holding her hand as they strolled down a quiet country lane. Only occasionally had he dared to kiss her in the shelter of the big oak tree; she'd only occasionally allowed it. But the walks always ended the same, with him escorting her safely to her parents' front door and leaving her there with a polite kiss on the cheek under her mother's watchful eye.

Looking up at him from under half-lidded eyes, Grace pressed her groin to his and twisted her hips slightly, rubbing up against him. "Never done this?"

His breath sucked in with a gasp, and although he was still holding her forearms, Nathan realized he wasn't pulling her hands away from his body. In fact his face was slowly inclining toward hers, his gaze riveted on her lips and the pink tip of her tongue darting out to lick them. As inevitable as the sun sinking into the western horizon his mouth was drawn back to hers. Misgivings and moral dilemmas still clattered around in his brain, but he was able to dull their noise and concentrate completely on her sweet lips yielding to his.

His mouth opened and closed against hers in little kisses. Nathan dared to let his tongue slip out to trace the shape of her lips. Grace's warm, wet tongue touched his and they explored each other tentatively at first then with growing urgency.

He slipped his arms around her, splaying his hands on her back and feeling her hot skin and the sharp points of her spine beneath the thin material of her dress. He moved his hands experimentally up and down the length of her back, stopping short of crossing the line from waist to buttocks.

Bonnie Dee

Grace had no such compunction. Her hands roamed restlessly on his back, feeling him through his T-shirt, before settling below his waist. Nathan emitted a surprised grunt when she grasped his bottom and squeezed. She pulled her mouth from his and kissed his jaw and neck.

"Too hot 'n' sticky here. Come on." She turned from him abruptly and taking his hand, led him along the path she'd made through the berry patch to the woods.

Chapter Three

With her eyes not holding him hostage and her lips not kissing his common sense away, Nathan's worries clamored to the surface. He should stop this now before it went any farther; tell the girl he must be on his way; extricate himself from this very dangerous situation before it was too late. But underneath the cool spread of tree branches, Grace looked up at him again and he was lost.

"I should... I have to..."

She lifted a hand and rested her fingers over his lips. "Shh. Tarry a while." She pulled him down to the ground with her. It was carpeted with long, feathery, dried pine needles that released a sharp tang as they were crushed beneath two bodies.

Sitting close to Nathan, Grace pressed her palms to his, measuring her small hands against his larger ones. Then she linked her purple-stained fingers with his, clasping their hands together.

He watched her hand play, so innocent and charming, and relaxed a little. This wasn't harmful and it would hurt no one if he kissed her once or twice. Suiting action to thought, Nathan leaned to kiss her once more. This time he pushed his hand into her tangled hair. The silky strands slipped and caught between his fingers. Underneath the wild mass he cupped the back of her fragile skull.

He breathed in her scent as he kissed her over and over. Her hair smelled of natural oils and her body, covered in a sheen of sweat, was musky and feminine. Her odor was ripe and rich as the earth, arousing him in a primal way that Mary Albright's fresh soap and floral perfume never had. As the kisses deepened, his tongue delving into Grace's mouth and twisting sinuously with hers, Nathan groaned quietly.

His left hand released hers and moved to rest on her rib cage. He could feel the ladder of bones beneath his palm and climbed it until he reached a soft mound. His heart, already pounding, jolted, missed a beat then raced even faster as his hand encountered its first female breast. Mary had never allowed this familiarity. Nathan fondled the soft, resilient bulge, testing its shape and weight and experimenting with rolling the hard, pointed nipple between his fingers. The thin fabric of Grace's dress was no hindrance to his exploration. She may as well have been nude he could feel her so well.

Nathan released her lips and trailed his mouth to her soft cheek then down to her throat. Her pulse beat against his lips as he nuzzled there and tasted the salt-sweat of her skin. He moved his hand to her other breast, squeezing lightly and teasing the nipple to sharpness with practiced ease now. His mouth skated around the curve of her neck to lick the soft spot just beneath her ear.

Grace laughed and squirmed, pushing her ear to her shoulder to shut him out.

Nathan was delighted at her reaction and at the musical sound of her laughter. He dove in to catch her on the other side, kissing and nibbling her neck while she shrieked and pushed him away.

He sat for a moment, regarding her flushed face and smiling mouth. The girl had all the grace and beauty of a wild creature. He reached out and pushed a lock of her hair back from her eye, tucking it around the pink shell of her ear. The light moment between them darkened to weighty significance as their eyes met and held. A charge of primitive desire passed between them from blue eyes to brown.

Nathan leaned in to kiss her again, and this time it wasn't a tentative exploration, but deep and possessive. Grace kissed him back, hungry and needy. Soft little moans rose from her throat driving him to greater heights of arousal. Her fingers clutched the material of his T-shirt over his chest, clinging like a burr.

His erection grew as their groping and kissing escalated. He shifted his body sideways until he could press his erection into her hip, but the slight friction didn't satisfy him.

Grace pulled away from their passionate kissing, breathing hard, her eyes wide open and glazed. She bunched Nathan's shirt up in both hands and tugged it over his head, casting it aside and staring at his sweaty, heaving chest. She reached out and laid her palm flat on it then stroked her hand down the planes of his chest and abdomen. His stomach muscles twitched violently beneath her caressing touch.

Nathan groaned again. He should stop her now. He could no longer pretend this was an innocent flirtation in the woods. A line was being crossed into an ethical and moral quagmire from which he couldn't hope to emerge clean. Still he hesitated, breathing sharply in and out as Grace's hand dragged slowly up, down and around his naked torso. Nathan prayed to God for the strength to grab her wrist and pull her hand away, to tell her what they were doing was wrong and must end.

Suddenly Grace drew back, and he sent a silent thank you to the heavens for the answer to his prayer.

But she took hold of the hem of her dingy cotton shift and pulled it up over her head, revealing her slim, nude body. Dark tufts of hair shadowed her armpits and her arms rose long and white as lilies. Her breasts were drawn up by the stretch of her arms, the nipples erect and a deep rose color against her pale bosom. They pointed straight at Nathan.

Taking her head out of the neck hole of the dress, she shook her hair back and looked at him.

Nathan's throat constricted and his chest hurt like someone had punched it. He could do nothing but stare and stare at her beautiful naked body, admiring all the curves and angles; her rounded shoulders and high, firm breasts, the delicate wings of her collarbones and the plane of her chest. Her stomach was flat and smooth and her waist nipped in then flared out at her hips in a pretty curve. Her sex was concealed by a pair of white underpants. Her legs sprawled across the pine needles as long and graceful as a young colt's.

His eyes focused on hers once more. "We mustn't do this," he murmured.

"Why not?" Her voice was a quiet whisper too. She cupped a hand underneath each breast and lifted them like an offering.

Nathan swallowed hard and searched his mind for the reason. He couldn't remember it. Leaning forward, he lowered his head to the level of her chest and kissed the soft skin at the top of her breast. His fingers replaced hers on the underside, caressing the delicate flesh. He kissed his way down the slope of her breast then slowly sucked the solid warmth of her nipple into his mouth. His tongue rolled over it and he suckled like a child.

Grace's hand slipped into his hair, holding his head to her. She moaned quietly and arched her chest into his mouth.

Nathan was surprised at her sounds of pleasure. He hadn't thought about women liking sexual things. Actually, he'd tried to keep his mind away from bodily matters entirely, focusing on higher, purer pursuits. But being a young man it was inevitable that in the dark of night in his solitary bed he would fantasize about sex, wondering what the act was really like and picturing female attributes; the curve of a calf, the glimpse of a pale inner arm, the bow of a full lip. He would stroke himself with his eyes squeezed tight shut, imagining what the bumps in the front of Mary Albright's dress might look like unclothed.

But this, the real thing, was so much stronger, headier, earthier than he could ever have imagined. He hadn't counted on the texture of flesh or the smell of it. And he hadn't expected the soft whimpers of pleasure a woman would make that sent a man's blood raging through his veins.

Nathan gave his attention to her other breast, stroking and fondling it before drawing the nipple between his lips and laving it with his tongue. The salty flavor of her skin was mixed with something else he couldn't identify—an essence that was simply her.

One of her hands tangled in his hair, the other caressed his shoulder, feeling his muscle then stroking down the length of his back as far as she could reach. She shifted and lay back on the ground.

Nathan followed her, lying cradled between her thighs, his erection pressed into her sex through layers of fabric. He thrust his hips, rubbing his hardness against her. She moaned and wiggled beneath him. His cock must be touching a spot that felt good to her too. He lowered his head to kiss her mouth once more, trying to decide if her berry-flavored lips or her breasts were softer.

When he'd transferred his attentions to her breast again, he decided he couldn't make a choice. Both parts of her were equally soft and perfect—as was the dip of her waist, the drum-taut skin of her stomach, her slender neck and rounded cheek. There wasn't a single feature of her body that wasn't supple, feminine and utterly delectable.

After petting and loving her breasts for a while, he moved lower, kissing down the surface of her stomach between the ridges of her rib cage and fluttering his lips over her bellybutton. Her stomach leaped and twitched as he kissed her there. He stopped when he reached the waistband of her underwear, staring for a moment. Dare he go further? Tentatively he cupped his hand over the hard mound of her pubic bone through the cotton fabric.

Grace rose to his touch, lifting her hips off the ground. Encouraged, he slid his hand across the hard bump and down the soft cleft in between her legs. Her underwear was damp and it occurred to him that it wasn't sweat but some mysterious womanly fluid. He exhaled, excited by the idea, and suddenly he desperately needed to feel that secret place between her legs without the barrier of fabric.

Nathan pressed another kiss to her stomach before stealing a glance at Grace's face.

Her eyes were closed and her chin lifted, her lips slightly parted.

He slipped his hand down inside her underwear to feel the wiry fluff of curls and slippery folds of her sex with his seeking fingers. Sliding them along her seam, he encountered the open entrance of her sex. Nathan didn't know what he'd expected to find between a woman's legs, but this was so different, so messy and real. It thrilled him. His cock swelled to its limit, vibrating and eager to be buried inside her hot depths.

Grace gasped at the intrusion of his fingers then let out another soft, whimpering moan that made Nathan want to answer with a growl.

He moved his fingers in and out of her where his throbbing cock wanted to be. The primitive need to possess her body rose in him in growing waves. It seemed fully possible he might tear her underpants off and impale her with his cock like a savage beast. He hadn't known he was capable of such violent urges.

The girl thrust up against his probing fingers. After a moment, she reached down and took hold of his hand, moving it farther up her slit, showing him where she wanted him. "Right there."

Beneath his finger, Nathan felt a small, hard nub. He tickled it lightly and the results were extravagant. Grace writhed and moaned. "More!" she gasped.

Nathan laid aside his own urgent need to concentrate on the fascinating phenomenon a simple rub with his finger could produce. In a few short moments Grace had moved from wiggling and moaning to bucking up against his circling finger. Her neck arched as her head fell back, and her body lifted off the piney mat like a bridge. She cried out, a guttural howl that sent another rage of desire through him then her body dropped back down to earth and she lay still, breathing heavily.

Nathan had come from the friction of his own stroking hand enough times to understand what had just happened to Grace. But no one had ever told him women could experience release like a man did. In his life, talk of sex had been limited. He knew it was for intended procreation, but sometimes men struggled against base needs that women could never understand. Grace's orgasm was a revelation.

He watched her face, sweating and pink-cheeked, as she came down into herself. Ragged breaths panted from her parted lips. Strands of hair clung to her damp forehead and her eyelashes fluttered against her cheeks. Suddenly her eyes opened and she gazed right at him. A slow smile curved her mouth.

He was as pleased as if he'd received a precious gift. He returned her smile.

Grace held her hand out toward him.

Although he knew it was too late to turn back, he asked, "Are you sure?"

She nodded and reached to pull her underpants down her hips.

Nathan rose and quickly took off his shoes, socks and pants while watching Grace shimmy her underwear off her legs. His focus was riveted on the dark triangle of hair at the apex of her thighs and the glimpse of woman parts between her legs. He drew a deep breath, bringing his racing heart back under control, and lowered himself on top of her. When he was cradled between her legs once more, there was no fabric trapping his penis and it nestled snugly between her slick folds of her labia.

He thrust against her, slow and easy for several strokes, just rubbing along her crevice. Then he reached down between them and positioned his cock at her opening. He could barely breathe and his body quivered with tension as he pushed into her and was enveloped in her wetness. The heat and friction of his entry into her body was exquisite. Nathan closed his eyes, immersing himself in the sensation.

Grace gasped aloud as he sheathed himself completely in her depths.

His eyes opened and he gazed at her in concern. "Have I hurt you?"

"Mm." She shook her head, her lips pressed in a tight line. "Just a little. I ain't done this before."

"What?" His eyes widened and he stilled inside her. "What?" Her manner had been so relaxed and assured as she initiated their lovemaking that he'd never considered she could be a virgin.

"It's all right." She slid her hands down his back and gripped his ass, pulling him tighter to her. "I want to."

"But..." He was frozen, torn between the towering need still throbbing in his cock and the ethical dilemma of having sex outside of marriage *and* with a virgin. His conscience sent signals to his dick and it flagged slightly at the news.

"Don't stop. Go ahead," she urged, lifting her hips and tightening her inner muscles around him.

"But why?"

She looked up at him and her eyes were dark wells of sadness. "I need to. Please."

Nathan felt like the world had tilted. The heat and light of the summer day still surrounded them, but unexpected shadows moved in it now. What had been a simple fulfillment of lust took on an aspect of something deeper and darker. He didn't know what Grace's sorrow was, only that he had the power to alleviate it. The question of morality faded from his mind and he turned his attention to giving her what she wanted.

"All right. If you're sure," he said quietly.

She caressed his naked flanks, encouraging him to move within her again.

Nathan pulled slowly out and eased back in, concentrating on controlling the glide in and out of her tight channel. His knees and hands dug into the ground through the prickle of pine needles and twigs. Sweat rolled down his back and face and gathered between their bodies. His stomach slid against hers, their flesh sticking together slightly from the sweat pooled between them. Nathan's jaw clenched as he forced himself to keep a steady, gentle pace when his body wanted to ram into her like an army assaulting a castle wall.

He leaned down to press a kiss to her cheek and whisper near her ear. "All right?"

"Yes." She lifted her hips to meet his thrusts and made a soft humming sound in her throat. Her hands slid up his sweat-slicked back to his shoulders and clung to him. She wrapped her legs around his hips, changing the angle of penetration, making it even deeper.

Nathan pumped into her faster as his arousal grew. The wet sounds their bodies made together and his harsh gasps and grunts floated through the still, humid air around them. Raw need like sensitive nerve endings in an open wound rampaged through him. He could no longer control his pace, but pressed into her slight body harder and deeper with each thrust. It felt wonderful, powerful and achingly painful as the separate strands of desire coiled together and twined into one strong throbbing chord of want.

Nathan's balls drew up tight and a shuddering began at the root of his cock. The sensation spilled through him to explode in a burst of pure euphoria as he pushed deep inside her and released. He felt himself rise from his body and float free for astounding moments before crashing back into the solidity of flesh.

God, I should be sorry, but I'm not. The fleeting thought darted through his mind then disappeared again, leaving him full of nothing but ecstasy.

Chapter Four

She held him to her as the last tremors of delight quivered through him. He turned his face into the crook of her neck and kissed her, breathing her in so he would remember this moment always. "Thank you," he murmured soundlessly.

Her hand rubbed his back, up and down in rhythmic strokes. "'Twas different than I expected," she said after a moment.

He lifted his face to look at her with a frown. "But all right?"

She met his eyes and smiled. "Yes. All right."

Nathan rolled off her body to lie beside her. Grace's backside must be raw from being scraped across a carpet of pine needles. He watched his red, glistening prick, slowly diminishing from its aroused state, then gazed at the thatch of hair hiding Grace's sex and the wonders it contained. Reaching out, he touched her, stroking his finger idly over the hard nub he'd discovered there.

She twitched and jerked away, squeezing her thighs together and laughing. Grabbing his wrist, she drew his hand up to hold it against her breast instead.

He studied her face, the large, dark eyes, pointed nose, firm little chin and bee-stung lips.

"Was it really all right?" His question was about more than her physical well-being. Now that the burst of rapture had faded, thorny moral questions rose in his mind again. "How old *are* you?" Lying there so thin and delicate, she appeared only thirteen or so.

"Nineteen." She regarded him with a twinkle in her eye. "Preacher, you worry too much. I done tole you it was all right. More'an that. It was good."

He couldn't stop questioning her. "Why? Why would you want to do this with a stranger?"

She shrugged. "The spirit moved me." Her eyelids lowered until they were almost closed. "Besides, I think you was sent to me today. Like an angel."

"What?" A chill went through him despite the heat. He was supposed to be a man of God, ministering to people's spiritual and psychological needs. Had he just taken advantage of a poor girl with romantic sacred delusions?

"When you asked about my family, I didn't tell you everything. My momma did used to read us from the Bible, but she died nigh on two years ago. My little sister, Shelly, got took by the same fever, and my older brother, Jake, lit off for the city shortly after. He couldn't stand livin' at the homeplace no more. So that left just Daddy an' me."

Nathan held his breath, listening to her quiet confession. His hand was still wrapped around her small, soft breast and he sheltered it in his palm, feeling her heartbeat.

Grace's eyes closed, the long, dark lashes fanning her cheeks. She drew a choked breath. "Then a couple months ago Daddy died too. He went huntin' and didn't come back for a few days. I went lookin' for him and found him at the bottom of a ravine. Edge musta crumbled away an' he fell. I climbed down, but he 'as already gone." Her jaw clenched tight. "Couldn't take

'im up so I went and got a shovel and buried him right there."
She opened her glistening eyes and looked at Nathan. "You
suspect that's all right? I said a prayer."

"Yes," he assured her. "I'm sure God heard you. You did
what you could. But why didn't you go get one of your
neighbors to help you?"

She frowned. "Nearest neighbor's couple miles away and
not too neighborly. Flies was already settin' in and I had to get
Daddy in the ground."

Nathan pictured the girl struggling with the monumental
task of digging a hole in the hard, stony mountain, and
surrendering her father's corpse into the earth. Grace was a
tough, resilient young woman. Her isolation and loneliness
moved him. "So you haven't talked to anyone about this, and
you've been living on your own ever since?"

"I get by. I got a garden. I fish and shoot game with Daddy's
rifle."

"But what will you do in winter? You can't stay up on the
mountain all alone. You should come down to the village.
People will help you."

Slipping out from beneath his hand, she sat up and
wrapped her arms around her knees. "I ain't used to people.
Don't know as I'd get on too well."

Nathan frowned and sat up too. What was holding her
here? She didn't seem shy to him. Perhaps she was simply
afraid of change. He touched her stiff shoulder. "What made
you think God sent me?"

Grace rested her cheek on her knee and looked at him. "I
was feelin' exceptional lonesome today. Missin' my family and
wantin' someone in a powerful way. I weren't prayin' exactly,
but wantin' with all my might for someone to come along—and

then there you was. 'Divine providence', my momma woulda said."

Nathan stroked her hair then pulled his hand away. "You needed someone to talk to not... I should have just talked to you. What kind of spiritual counselor am I?"

"No." She lifted her head and turned toward him. "Not just talkin'. I wanted exactly what you give me. All of that." She took his hand in hers and gazed into his eyes, quoting in a low voice, "'My beloved is all radiant and ruddy, distinguished among ten thousand. His head is the finest gold, his locks are wavy. His speech is most sweet and he is altogether desirable.' You know that? It's from the Bible."

"Yes. I know it." Nathan had steered clear of the Song of Solomon since most of the verses tended to enflame a young man's senses, but he recognized the opulent words of love.

Grace blushed and looked down at their joined hands. "Ain't sayin' you're my beloved or nothin'. But what we did made me feel good like that—warm and alive again."

Nathan enfolded her in his arms, pulling her across his lap and holding her close. "It was very special. And it was my first time too," he admitted. Resting his chin on the top of her head, he brushed stray pine needles and grit from her hair and back. "I'm sorry about your family. Losing all of them like that is very hard. It's difficult to see God's hand in it."

She nodded, her warm head moving against his neck. His arm fit snugly around her middle and she clasped it with both hands. "I don't understand it, but there's gotta be a reason for everythin', don't you think?"

"Yes." He kissed her hair, and when she tilted her head back to look up at him, kissed her lips. "Yes. Guess I wouldn't be in this line of work if I didn't believe that." He smiled.

Grace smiled back then wrapped her arms around his neck and held tight, nuzzling her mouth into the crook of his neck and shoulder.

He held her for a long while before she spoke again. "Feels awful nice like this, but kind of hot an' sticky. Mayhap we should wash up at the stream." She rose from his lap, and Nathan stood too. They walked through the trees as natural as Adam and Eve in the garden to kneel once more by the spot where the water welled up from the ground. It trickled along a narrow streambed that meandered off into the woods.

Grace immersed her face in the water and splashed it all over her chest and arms. She threw handfuls over her shoulders onto her back and washed between her legs. The sight of her, wet and dripping, stirred Nathan's desire again. He looked away until she was finished then took his turn at the water. When he was done bathing in the icy water, he sat back on his heels, refreshed.

Grace had her hands behind her head, plaiting her long hair into a braid. He watched with fascination her quick, efficient movements, the rise and fall of her breasts as her arms stretched behind her head, the lift of her rib cage and the way her mouth pursed a little as she concentrated on the task. She fastened the end of the braid with a piece of string then glanced at Nathan. "Shoulda had my hair up all day. It's too hot to have it stragglin' down."

"Looked pretty though." He reached out and touched the thick plait lying across her shoulder. "Looks pretty like that too."

Her smile lit up her eyes. Nathan's heart twisted and he realized right then he might be in trouble. It would be too easy to move from lust to love with such a sweet, pretty girl, who'd given herself without hesitation, opening up a world of pleasure to him.

He stood, offering his hand to her this time. "Maybe we should go back to blackberry picking. See if we can fill those pails before the sun goes down."

Chapter Five

They walked back to where their clothes lay discarded underneath the pine trees and dressed. Nathan had sometimes wondered how married couples managed to interact so politely and casually in front of people when they did such intimate, private things together in bed at night. He had imagined it would be strange to be naked in front of his bride on their wedding night and to face her the next morning after having sex, but it wasn't strange at all with Grace. He didn't feel shy or awkward around her—and he barely knew her.

As they returned to the berry patch, she talked about some of the other families on the mountain; the hot-tempered Cadeys, the shiftless Lowes and the kindhearted but extremely luckless Stantons. While they picked, she told him stories about people in the community and the intricate relationships between the various families. Nathan felt he'd gleaned more information from listening to Grace than if he'd tramped all over the mountain. Of course, eventually he had to make contact with everyone, but this afternoon hadn't been completely squandered on selfish pursuits.

Grace questioned him about what it was like growing up in the north and he told her all about his boyhood in Michigan, his family, friends, school and life at the seminary.

"How about you?" he asked. "Did you attend school or learn at home?"

"My momma taught us our letters. The Bible is the only book we got, but my daddy was a great storyteller. My brother, Jack, was too. I wish'd he'd come back."

"Where did he go?"

"Lexington. Leastways that's where he and Hiram was headed." She topped off her bucket with a final berry then set it aside. "Hiram was Jack's friend and my beau for a while 'til they took off."

"Oh." That explained some things, like how Grace seemed so comfortable with her body and his. She'd had a boyfriend and they fooled around some.

"He never understood me though. He was a real lunkhead."

Nathan smiled, glad to hear it. "My girlfriend back home was named Mary," he offered.

"She waitin' for you there?" Grace pressed her hands against the small of her back and arched it, which thrust her breasts forward fetchingly.

"No. She married someone else from our high school class while I was off at college." He shrugged. "Just as well. We really didn't have much in common."

She walked over to where he was picking and began helping him fill his pail. "Guess you have a lot of girls back in your hometown who'd be glad to hitch up with a preacher."

He shrugged again. It was true. In the brief time he'd spent at home after graduation his mother had invited a half dozen unmarried young ladies to dinner to meet "my son, the minister".

The shadows of the trees spread over the glade bringing relief from the unrelenting sun. The late afternoon slant of sunlight gave Nathan a melancholy feeling of time slipping away. His bucket was almost filled.

His hand brushed against Grace's as both of them dropped berries into the pail at the same time. They looked up and their eyes met.

Nathan lowered his bucket to the ground then straightened and put his hands on her waist. He pulled her close and bent to kiss her. She tasted sweet as the berries she'd been eating. He savored her lips, flicking his tongue lightly over them and probing into her mouth to meet her tongue. Her mouth was wet and warm as a summer's day.

He didn't mean for things to escalate. He knew their afternoon together was drawing to a close and only wanted to share a few kisses before they went their separate ways. But one kiss led to another, each deeper and more urgent.

Grace combed her fingers through his hair and held his head, drawing him down to her. Her mouth was open and seeking, kissing him with a passion and intensity that stole his breath. She released his head and moved her hands down to his stomach, pushing them up underneath his shirt.

Not again, he thought, feeling his resistance drain away beneath the assault of her stroking hands. *I shouldn't. She's vulnerable. I'm compromising her virtue. I'm a minister for God's sake.*

Too late. With a strangled groan, he ripped his shirt over his head and tossed it on top of a clump of blackberry canes, then grabbed Grace's shift and tugged.

She raised her arms so he could pull it off her. When he had thrown it aside, Nathan took hold of her wrists and ran his hands the entire length of her upraised arms down her sides to her waist. He loved the long line of her body and the way she shivered at his touch. Bringing his hands up to her breasts, he kneaded the round globes, toying with her nipples. He experimented with pulling lightly and twisting them. The way Grace thrust her chest into his hands and cried out softly let him know she liked it.

Nathan bent his head to draw one of the beaded nipples into his mouth.

"Wait," Grace said. She reached into the blackberry leaves behind her and brought her hand out with a juicy indigo berry.

In a flash, he knew what she was going to do and the knowledge sent a hot jolt of yearning to his already erect penis. It swelled harder, straining against his pants.

Grace held the blackberry just above her nipple and squeezed. Juice trickled from the mashed pulp onto the erect bud.

Nathan emitted a soft, animal growl deep in his throat. He leaned to lap up the dripping juice then sucked her sweetened nipple into his mouth. It tasted like pure nectar, like the very essence of this sultry August day. He rolled his tongue over the turgid flesh and sucked hard.

Grace moaned and pushed toward him, clasping his head to her breast.

When he had licked and sucked every last drop of the sticky juice from one breast, he turned his attention to the other. Once more Grace anointed her breast with berry juice, coating the tip with not only juice but the pulpy flesh of the fruit as well.

Enraptured with the exotic experience, Nathan dropped to his knees and lapped and suckled her juicy breast like a starving man. He splayed one hand on her back, holding her close, and fondled her breast with the other. He glanced up to see Grace looking down at him through half-closed eyes. Her lips were parted and her breathing heavy.

Nathan moved his mouth to just below her breast and kissed the hard bone of her rib cage. He licked, nibbled and kissed every inch of her abdomen right down to the edge of her underpants. Then he slid the drawers down her hips and off her legs.

He crouched before her, his eyes level with her sex. He hadn't been able to look at it too closely before, being much more intent on getting inside it, but now Nathan took the opportunity to examine the mystery of her womanhood, the "cradle of life" that drove men wild. Tentatively, he petted the tuft of hair covering her pubic mound. He rifled his fingers through it then separated the plump pink folds beneath to reveal the hard little nub he had played with earlier. It rose erect and red from a little hood of flesh. When he brushed the tip of his finger over it, Grace jerked. Her reaction made him smile.

Nathan delved his fingers farther down her slick, wet vulva and parted the folds of flesh with his thumbs. He looked at the reddened flesh surrounding her dark entrance.

Grace held absolutely still as he examined her down there.

Possessed by a primitive desire, he leaned in and licked lightly over the little button that brought her such delight. It tasted musky and slightly salty.

"Oh!" Grace's hands slipped into his hair and held his head. Her hips thrust forward as he continued to lap over the sensitive nerve bundle.

Blindly, Nathan reached for the bucket of berries sitting on the ground nearby. He pulled away from Grace for a moment and she whined in frustration. Excited at his creativity and daring, he mashed one of the softened berries against the sharp, red bud. Juice trickled down, following the folds of her sex.

Nathan bent his head and lapped up the seam, sampling the mingled flavor of sweet fruit and womanly juices. With no shame or hesitation he gave himself over to feasting on Grace's sex. She moaned and cried out, fisting her hands in his hair, as he continued to lick her labia then suck and nibble her clitoris.

With a loud cry she bucked against his mouth. He slipped his tongue down her slit to her entrance once more and realized from the fresh gush of fluid that she had come. With his mouth, he'd brought her to orgasm. Nathan had never imagined such a thing was possible. He held her hips firmly between his hands, keeping her from tumbling to the ground since her quivering legs could barely hold her upright.

Rising to his feet, he enfolded her in his arms. She leaned her head on his chest, panting and gasping. Her arms were around his back, clutching his shoulders from behind.

Nathan was ready to take her right there, standing in the middle of the briar patch, but the threat of thorns stopped him. "Come on," he whispered, pulling her arms from around him and taking her hand.

Leading her back to the trees at the edge of the glade, he took off the rest of his clothes and backed her up to the widest tree trunk he could find. He lifted her with a hand under each buttock and moved in between her legs, pressing her against the tree. His cock found its own way to her slick entrance without his hand to guide it. With a grunt, Nathan pushed inside her hot channel.

Her legs wrapped around his waist holding him to her, fingers gripping his shoulders almost painfully. Luminous eyes gazed into his as he drove his cock into her again and again. Her full bottom lip caught between her teeth and she made little soft sounds.

Nathan was suddenly concerned that the rough bark of the tree was scraping her back. "Are you all right?"

She nodded. "Keep going. Harder."

The word "harder" came out low and rough. The raw need in her voice sent a wildfire of arousal blazing through him. He shifted his feet farther apart, planting them more firmly on the uneven ground and did as she bid. His jaw clenched with the effort of pumping his hips and supporting her weight. Her body clenched around his dick as he pushed in and out. The friction was amazing, sending waves of pleasure coursing through his nervous system. It took only minutes for him to reach climax. Abruptly, like a string of firecrackers one leading to the next, his synapses fired and his orgasm exploded in a powerful burst.

Nathan drove into Grace's body with a wordless cry. His fingers dug into the soft globes of her bottom and he collapsed against her, his face pressed to her shoulder. *I will remember this always—this afternoon, this moment, this woman. When I'm old and shivering by my fireside in the dead of winter, I'll remember this scorching August day and making love to a beautiful woman beneath a tree.*

He blew out a shaky breath and drew in another. Lifting his head, he looked into Grace's eyes.

She smiled at him, a sweet, trembling, little smile.

He eased his cock out of her and lowered her to her feet, holding her until she got her balance. Turning her around, he ran his hand over her back, feeling the abrasions from the tree bark. "I'm sorry."

She glanced at him over her shoulder and smiled. "It don't hurt. Anyway, I liked it. 'Twas somethin' powerful."

Taking her by the shoulders and facing her toward him again, he kissed her then rested his forehead against hers. "This whole day was somethin' powerful."

"Guess it's over now though. Sun's gettin' low." Grace stepped away from him as he released her.

Nathan saw she was right. He was surprised as always by the sudden changes in the mountains. Right now the light had the golden, glowing quality of very late afternoon, but soon it would be gone. Once the sun set behind the mountains, the land quickly plunged into deep gray twilight then blackness. "We'd better get dressed."

Once more they located their scattered clothes and put them on. Nathan picked up both of the full buckets of berries and faced Grace. "Do you want me to see you home?"

"If you do, you won't make it back to the valley before dark."

Nathan understood an offer was being made. If he went with Grace, he would stay the night at her house. When he returned to the rectory in the morning, there would be questions about where he'd spent his night on the mountain. He could lie and say he'd gotten lost and had to sleep in the woods or he could tell the truth and set tongues wagging about the preacher and the Parkins girl.

Even if his stay with her was innocent, people would talk and the slowly developing respect of the congregation for a minister considered "too young" would be damaged.

Besides which, Nathan could feel the basic attraction between them rapidly blossoming into something deeper. He sensed the possibility of a relationship that would change the entire course of his life if he chose that path. Grace was nothing like the pretty, accomplished, acceptable, Christian girl he expected to marry. He couldn't get involved with someone like her—not for more than one summer afternoon.

Looking down at the berries, he offered the buckets to her. "I guess I'd better be getting back to the parsonage. Mrs. Crowder will have dinner ready."

She accepted the pails. "All right then." She looked past him down the mountain. "You can find your way home all right?"

Nathan gazed into the dark depths of her eyes. "Yes. Thank you... Thank you for everything. I'm sorry I couldn't see you home."

She nodded and gave him a wistful smile. "That's all right. I thank you for everything too. You lit up my day some." With that she turned and walked away from him into the woods.

Nathan stared after her for a moment. The leaves swayed at her passing then were still. It was as if she'd never been there. He flexed his hands by his sides and lifted one to examine a long, red scratch on the back of it. Sighing, he headed down the mountain toward the parsonage.

Chapter Six

That night Nathan lay in his rumpled bedcovers, clad only in his underwear, one hand splayed across his naked chest. The blackberry scratches on his hands and arms itched and the room was too hot and stuffy for sleep. He closed his eyes and commanded himself to sleep, but images from his day on the mountain played against the back of his eyelids like a moving picture.

He couldn't get Grace out of his mind. Not only their sexual encounters, but the things she'd said, the way she moved, everything about her. She was unlike any woman he'd ever met. She was a force of nature, basic and elemental, but with glimmers of quick wit and humor showing a keen mind despite her lack of formal education.

But when he tried to picture her anyplace besides the mountain, he couldn't imagine it. He couldn't see her, for example, sitting in a front pew at church wearing a Sunday hat. The idea of her socializing with the church ladies or singing in the choir seemed ludicrous. He absolutely couldn't place her at his family's table for Christmas dinner, eating off his mother's best china and making polite conversation with his parents.

He could, however, imagine her sharing his bed at night. He could imagine that all too well.

With a frustrated groan, he climbed out of bed and went to the window. A three-quarter moon shone in the dark night. It reflected off the roofs of houses and the tops of trees so they shimmered all the way up the mountain. He could see the ridge where he'd met Grace. She was up there somewhere, tucked away in her bed in a little mountain shack, alone, as he was alone.

Nathan cursed himself. He'd been so caught up in the idea of whether or not he should go with Grace that he'd completely overlooked his pastoral duty. Knowing about her father's death, he should have continued to encourage her to come down from the mountain and find a place in the town. The harsh mountain life was no good for a woman alone. Whatever his feelings for her, whatever they'd done, it was his responsibility to make sure the girl was cared for and brought into the communal fold. Tomorrow he would go back, find her and fulfill that obligation.

But when Nathan woke the next day, other duties claimed his attention. There was a baby born early whose fragile life hung in the balance. He went to pray with the young parents for a while in the morning. Then there was a ladies' guild luncheon he'd promised to attend. Following that he consulted with the curate about an infestation of carpenter ants in the church building. It was midafternoon by then and Nathan had not prepared his Sunday sermon.

Grace was still in his mind as she had been all day, teasing around at the edges of his consciousness, so he wrote his sermon on the topic of "grace". His thoughts were unruly and the writing went slow, and soon it was too late in the day to trek up the mountain.

As he stood by his bedroom window that night and looked at the black silhouette of the ridge against the midnight blue sky, he swore he would go the next day right after church.

Nathan's sermon that Sunday morning was lackluster at best. He stumbled over his words and had trouble delivering them with conviction. He felt like a sham in his black clerical garb, facing a roomful of people who'd experienced much more of the joys and suffering of life than he had. Who was he to tell them anything? God's grace, blessing and soothing their way, sounded beautiful in theory, but how did the words really help someone who'd lost a loved one or was suffering an illness. Suddenly, everything about his speech seemed impractical and useless.

Nathan closed his eyes and drew a breath before speaking to his congregation again. "I believe in God's grace, but I know sometimes it's hard to feel it when things are very bad in your life. I believe that grace may come to a person in a much more concrete form than they expect; maybe a neighbor's helpfulness, a kind word spoken by a friend or a loving gesture from a stranger. I think that is how God shows his grace in a very direct way that human beings can understand."

He looked around the church at the many pairs of eyes—all watching him for a change. After trying to think of something else to add, he ended his sermon simply. "That's what I believe."

As Nathan greeted the parishioners exiting the church building, Mrs. Grassle reminded him that he was invited to her family's home for Sunday dinner. She presented her daughter, Mae Ann, whom Nathan had already met several times. "You remember Mae Ann, Reverend? She makes a wonderful peach cobbler which we'll be having for dessert."

He shook the girl's hand. "I'm looking forward to it." He glanced up at the mountain looming over the valley church. After dinner with the Grassles, he would go.

When the last of the congregation had left the building, Nathan walked back to the parsonage to take off the choking clerical collar for a while and unwind before he had to socialize with the Grassles.

The moment he entered the front door he smelled it, sweet, rich and palpable as though he was tasting instead of smelling it. Hot blackberries.

On the dining room table sat a pie, the crust a pale brown and neatly fluted around the edges. He leaned down and breathed in the luscious aroma then rested his hand on the surface of the pie. It was still warm.

"Mrs. Crowder," he called, but there was no answer. It was her day off and he hadn't really expected her to be in the house. He knew she hadn't baked the pie. He knew where it came from.

A square of paper protruded from beneath the pie tin. He reached down and pulled out a note written in carefully printed letters on a square of cardboard cut from a soap flake box. "One day, like a crown of jewels, I will wear throughout my life. Better is one day than a lifetime of sorrowed nights."

His chest ached. He swallowed and read the words of the psalm again...and again. Breathing in the scent of warm blackberries, he flashed on every moment of the afternoon he'd spent with Grace, recalling the texture of her skin and hair, the smoothness and perfection of her breasts and body, and the smell and taste of her sex. He could hear her voice, rising and falling like bird song and her laughter bubbling like the stream of water in the forest. But mostly he thought of her eyes—the glint of mischief in them and the sorrow in their dark depths.

Nathan set the note down on the table and touched the pie again. Still warm. And she had left it while he was at church so she couldn't be far, maybe only halfway up the mountain. He could catch her if he hurried.

Spinning away from the table, he ran out the door into the bright sunlight. A pair of young boys were walking across the churchyard and he beckoned them over. "Please do me a favor. Stop by the Grassle's house and tell them I won't be able to make Sunday dinner. An emergency has come up."

"Yes, sir." Looking relieved as if they'd expected to be scolded for something, the two boys trotted off.

Nathan turned and walked briskly toward the road leading up the mountain. When he was out of sight of the church, he broke into a trot and after several paces a flat-out run. He raced up the slope, a line from the Song of Solomon reverberating with his thudding footsteps, "I am my beloved's and her desire is for me. Come, my beloved, and let us go forth into the fields. There I will give you my love."

He ran until he had a stitch in his side and his heart pounded painfully. Turning off on a dirt track, he skidded on a loose stone and almost fell to his knees, then he was off and running again, racing upward toward his beloved.

He rounded a bend in the path and saw a slight figure in the shadows of the trees ahead. For the blink of an eye he saw it as a wild creature, a doe which had wandered out of the woods. His eyes focused and he beheld the figure as a graceful female form walking along the road.

"Grace!"

She stopped and turned. Even from a distance he could see her eyes sparkle and light up on seeing him.

"Wait!" He ran toward her. "Wait for me."

She ran to meet him and slammed into his arms with a force that nearly knocked him off his feet, throwing her arms around him.

He held her slim body tight and buried his face in her hair, breathing her in. She smelled like woman and sweat, and around her like a precious perfume floated the lingering, sweet aroma of blackberry pie.

About the Author

Whether you're a fan of contemporary, paranormal or historical romance, you'll find something to enjoy among my books. My style is down to earth and my characters will feel like well-known friends by the time you've finished reading. I'm interested in flawed, often damaged, people who find the fulfillment they seek in one another. I live a quiet life with my family completely the opposite of my characters' adventures.

To learn more about Bonnie Dee, please visit http://bonniedee.com. Send an email to Bonnie Dee at bondav40@yahoo.com or join her Yahoo! group newsletter at http://groups.yahoo.com/group/Bonniedee.

Look for these titles by
Bonnie Dee

Now Available:

Finding Home
Evolving Man
Opposites Attract
Perfecting Amanda
The Valentine Effect

Coming Soon:

The Countess Takes a Lover
The Final Act

Liaisons in Jubilee

Jamie Craig

Chapter One

It took all of Katie's concentration not to glance at the clock on the wall. The meeting with the execs from New York was running late, they knew it was running late, and they knew Katie knew it was running late. None of them seemed to care. All three men were more interested in their bottom lines than their numb bottoms, and Katie was left smiling and making promises left and right about how this summer was going to be their biggest yet, no holds barred. If anyone noticed that her foot never stopped tapping beneath her chair, nobody said a word.

Twenty minutes later, Katie rose to shake their hands as they prepared to file out. Her mouth felt like it was stuck in Miss America mode.

"Good work, Katherine."

Smiling at Quentin Collins, her immediate superior, was far easier than dealing with the three men at the same time. He had been the one to recruit her from the Miami resort where she'd worked after graduating from USC, and it had been his influence that pulled her up through the ranks, until she was now the executive manager for the largest resort on the east coast. The holiday division of Jubilee Hotels was now in a position to become a major player in the international market.

Katie Mayes wanted to be the reason they got vaulted to the big leagues.

"I just want to get past the launch next weekend," she said, squaring her folder against the conference-room table. "Hothouse and the Guild both start tomorrow, but as far as I've been able to find out, they're not even half-booked."

"Which bodes well for us." His weathered face creased even further as he maneuvered toward the open doorway. "Keep it up, and all the sacrifices you've made for the team the past few years will be worth it. I promise."

Her grateful response was ready on her tongue, but the sudden appearance of Rosaria, her assistant, poking her head inside the room cut her off.

"Caleb's on the phone again," she said. "He got me to admit you didn't have any meetings after this one, and now he's insisting he needs to see you for dinner to discuss the launch entertainment program."

All the good will accrued from Quentin's comments vanished in the space of a heartbeat. Of all the people Rosaria could mention, it had to be Caleb Beckett. To everybody else, Caleb was just the Entertainment Director for the resort. Quentin knew the truth, though. He knew that Katie had indulged in an affair with Caleb for the three previous summers running, torrid four-month flings that ended as soon as the resort closed, only to resume as soon as the staff reconvened the next year. But it was also Quentin who had pulled her aside the week before she'd flown to Atlantic City.

"I know about you and Beckett," he said without preamble. When her mouth opened to try and explain, he shook his head. "Don't. I'm doing this now because I like you, Katherine. I think you've got a tremendous future with Jubilee. But you're a

manager and Beckett's your subordinate. You know better than anyone that company policy forbids your involvement with him."

She did. That's why she and Caleb had agreed to keep the affair secret. Well, that, and because it seemed to give their fucking an added edge knowing what was at risk if they got caught. Which, apparently, now they had.

"Nobody else knows," Quentin continued. "So I'm giving you a choice. Your job or your relationship. You can't have both."

As far as ultimatums went, it had been a fair one. That was why she'd deliberately avoided any but the barest of contact with Caleb since arriving at the hotel a month earlier. They saw each other in passing, or in meetings, or when she had to check on something in Entertainment, but every time he attempted to initiate something more private, Katie blew him off.

Just like she was going to do now.

"Find out what he wants and offer him a ten-minute block in Monday's staff meeting," she told Rosaria. "If he takes it, amend the agenda."

Rosaria nodded, scurrying off to leave them alone again. Out of the corner of her eye, Katie saw Quentin smile, though he didn't say a word as he headed for the doorway.

Inwardly, she sighed. It was a good thing she was done for the day. She was going to need a stiff drink to get over the headache blossoming behind her eyes.

౭౦౭౦౭౦

The night was sweltering by the time Katie was able to slip away. Neon painted the boardwalk in dancing red and yellow lights, and tourists were thick along the paths as they strolled along, clogging the way for those who had an actual destination in mind. In her low-slung jeans and silk camisole, Katie melted into the crowd, indiscernible even to locals as the sharp-suited executive manager at the Jubilee. She'd left the updo back at the hotel too. Her pale blonde hair hung in layers past her shoulders, highlighting the classical angles of her face even more effectively than her natural makeup and sheer pink lipstick. The combination made her look a good decade younger than her thirty-two years.

It took ten minutes of brisk walking to reach the nightclub she had in mind. The Wooden Nickel was good for escaping the rigors of her structured life. Nobody knew her here; for the most part, it catered to out-of-town college kids. Even better, it had a dance floor that spilled out onto the beach, and in the rising summer heat, it was better to be writhing under a clear, starry sky, than jammed into a small square with a hundred other bodies trying to do the same thing.

The club was already packed by the time Katie arrived. The air pulsated, the driving bass booming over the speakers, but she ignored the call of the music to head straight for the bar. She wanted a beer first. Something to get the juices flowing. Then she'd pick out her partner of the night and get the party started right.

It happened as she leaned over the counter to give the bartender her drink order.

Sweat dripped between her breasts, but it was the distinct prickle on the back of her neck that made Katie stiffen. Somebody was watching her. More than one set of eyes had followed her in, but this was different. This was watching with purpose. Easing back onto her stool as casually as possible, she tilted her head in the vague direction she'd sensed it.

Nobody was there. Nobody she knew, anyway. Then she lifted her gaze upward to the balcony railing that overlooked the beach.

Eyes like dark chocolate regarded her from beneath heavy lids. Dark brown hair he always wore too long for company policy—that he only got away with because he played on a regular basis with the bands he booked—was pushed back off his structured features, and some time over the past few weeks he'd grown a moustache and goatee that framed his succulent mouth perfectly. He even wore the dark suit and jewelry that typified his attire when he was onstage. Only Caleb Beckett had the aplomb and style to pull off such an ensemble in a college bar.

Katie's stomach alternated between constant fluttering and utter stillness. Damn it. She didn't need this tonight. If she had half a brain, she'd forget her drink, walk out of the club and go back to Jubilee.

It took everything she had to turn back to the bartender when he set her beer down in front of her. One drink. Then she'd leave.

She drank her beer quickly, the cold liquid temporarily soothing her parched throat, the alcohol going straight to her head. But it wasn't fast enough. She felt him at her back, even though he wasn't quite touching her.

"Come here to dance?"

It didn't matter if Caleb was speaking or singing. There was a velvet lilt to his voice that always sent a rush of warm electricity down the back of her neck. It might have been weeks since she'd felt him so close, months since she'd had him even closer, but the absence did nothing to lessen her body's reaction to his presence. If anything, it seemed to have made it stronger. Her pussy clenched, and her skin heated, and she had to fight not to lean back against the hard wall of his body right then and there.

Caleb still hadn't moved by the time she set down her empty bottle. "Brilliant deduction," she said, twisting around on her stool. He only moved enough not to get knocked over by her long legs, but it was still too close for Katie's comfort. Resting her elbows against the bar, she looked anywhere but at his hungry eyes. "The crowd looks lively tonight. Lucky for me."

Caleb never looked away from her. She could almost feel the weight of his eyes. "Do you think anybody here could keep up with you?"

"Does it matter?" She risked a glance back at him, only to get caught by the sight of his full mouth. How many times had she lost herself while kissing him? Too many to count. The sudden thought of what his newly acquired facial hair would feel like against her inner thigh made her cheeks flame, and Katie jerked her attention back to the thrashing crowd. "It's just dancing. It's not like I'm taking the guy home to fuck his brains out."

"Oh, it's never just dancing with you, Katie." He leaned forward. "But if that's what you want, I'll give you a few turns around the floor." Caleb smiled, managing to look charming and not at all lecherous. "Maybe you'll change your mind about the second part."

She faltered for a fraction of a second. It was tempting—*so* tempting. She'd never known a man to move like Caleb, in and out of bed, and after all, it was just a dance, no matter what he might profess. Except there was her job to consider, and she was his boss, and any concession now had the possibility of being disastrous later.

Katie slid off the stool and met his gaze without wavering. "I'm not going to change my mind," she said. He stood so close that their bodies brushed against each other as she headed for the dance floor. She didn't need to find a partner before she got there. Experience told her she wouldn't be alone for long once she started moving.

She watched Caleb from the corner of her eye as he slipped onto the dance floor. She tried to avoid him, but he adjusted his body, weaving with the rhythm and sliding between the writhing bodies that surrounded her. He positioned himself behind her, gripping her hips lightly.

It felt like the air had been sucked out of her lungs. Though her first instinct was to push him away, Katie knew that would start a scene she wasn't prepared to follow through with. Coming to the Wooden Nickel might give her a measure of anonymity, but if she got involved in a commotion, it would spread along the boardwalk faster than wildfire. And she knew Caleb. He wouldn't let something like attracting attention stop him. Hell, he was a performer at heart. He'd take that attention and use it to his advantage.

So she went with it. She didn't have a choice. Within seconds, though, the heat of the room and the throb of the music and the buzz from the beer made her initial concerns dissolve away. Her arm coiled up and around to caress Caleb's neck, her eyes fluttering shut so that she could focus on the pure physical pleasure suffusing her body. Caleb knew exactly how to fit against her, and somehow, knowing they were his hands holding her against him just spurred Katie to grind her ass back into his burgeoning erection.

Caleb followed her lead on the floor, and to her surprise, kept his hands firmly on her hips, instead of allowing them to wander over her curves. His body was so hot against hers and it was impossible not to let her mind drift to the very thing she said she wasn't going to do. But for the moment, she was happy to dance with him, to feel the rhythm of his hips, to feel the life pulsing from him with each step.

The music shifted from the upbeat tempo to something slow and sensual. Caleb tightened his grip and began directing her, leading her into the new tempo.

Gradually, Katie became aware of the other guys drifting away, and she opened her eyes to the swirling lights, wondering what in hell she was doing. So what if Caleb moved like liquid fire against her? So what if she felt like she was going to explode just from the firm caress of his hands? She was asking to get burned by letting him do this.

Twisting in his arms, Katie meant to walk away, but his searing gaze kept her pinned against his chest, just as effectively as his hard hands. She leaned forward, her breasts crushing to him with a familiar ache, and settled her mouth at his ear. It took a moment to say the words. His scent made her mouth go dry and she had to swallow more than once in order to find her voice again.

"Quentin knows," she breathed.

"So? Is he the jealous sort?" Caleb joked. When she didn't smile, the light in his eyes dimmed, and he managed to look like he might be taking this seriously. "What did he say to you?"

"He gave me an ultimatum. You or my job." She couldn't resist. It only took turning her head the scantest of inches to trail her mouth along his jaw. "You think anything else could've kept me away?"

Caleb wrapped his arm around her, rotating his hips and grinding against her. His other hand slid between her thighs to brush along her pussy, before moving up again to cup her ass and hold her closer to him. Tilting his head, he brushed his lips over her neck and said, "That's a very serious threat. Maybe you should go."

"Maybe I should."

But now that his arms were around her and it wasn't just his hands holding her in place, Katie was having a hard time remembering why she couldn't at least enjoy the dance with him. His body was strong and warm, his mouth sinful, and following his lead was as easy as breathing. She closed her eyes to let the music wash over them, her fingers threading through the long strands of his hair, and when she felt him kiss her neck again, Katie shivered.

"Miss me?" she murmured.

"Yes." He kissed a trail along her jaw. "I missed your mouth, and I missed your ass, and I missed the way you shout my name." He rested his lips on the corner of her mouth. They swayed to the music, not even an inch separating their bodies. "I think about you, think about holding you like this. Do you think about me?"

"Maybe." *Yes.* "Maybe there's nights when I get done with work and my feet start heading for your place before I can tell them to stop." *Maybe I get to your door before I talk myself into turning around.* "And maybe when I'm lying in my bed at night, the only way for me to come using my vibe is to pretend it's you."

The music stopped, but Katie didn't move. His breath fanned across her cheek, and she parted her lips to let her tongue dart out and taste the texture of his skin. The soft rasp of his moustache tickled, making her mouth water, and she exhaled, long and soft and slow as the need for him shuddered through her. "Maybe I should tell Quentin to mind his own fucking business."

Caleb began guiding her off the dance floor, but not quickly. "I think that's exactly what you should tell him. Come up to the balcony with me. I think we can find a private spot there."

She couldn't delude herself into thinking that staying at the club would keep her hands off him, but at the very least, it would keep their fucking to a minimum. And really, she hadn't sought Caleb out. She couldn't be blamed for it. They were colleagues who had run into each other in a public place, and if they were seen together, it was easily explained as coincidence.

But she was going to make sure they weren't seen. And maybe this would slake her thirst for him, at least temporarily.

Lacing her fingers through Caleb's, Katie shot him a wicked grin when he glanced down at their hands. "Someplace dark," she agreed, hoping he would take the hint. "I'll let you lead the way."

It seemed that everybody at the Wooden Nickel was there to dance. The balcony was virtually empty. They wound through the tables and chairs, moving farther into the shadows and farther from the bustling crowd. As soon as they were alone in a secluded corner, Caleb pushed her against the wall and claimed her mouth. His hands immediately sought her skin, pushing beneath her camisole to cup her breasts.

Katie smiled into the rough caress of his kiss, her hands finding their own paths to touch his enflamed skin. "You act like you've never had me alone before," she taunted, sliding her hands beneath his jacket to pull the white T-shirt he wore under it free of his waistband. She traced around to his belt buckle, letting her nails scrape along the way. "Better slow down. This time's going to have to last the both of us."

Caleb hissed, his palms rough against her nipples. His mouth was frantic and hungry, going from her lips, to her jaw, to her neck and back again, like he couldn't taste enough of her. "For a few minutes until I get you home?"

The raw desire in his voice made Katie cocky. Palming his cock through his pants, she whispered against his mouth, "Who said I was going home with you?"

"Did you say you weren't?" Caleb unbuttoned her jeans, pushing his fingers between her thighs. His sigh was full of satisfaction as he came in contact with her hot flesh. "Because I don't remember hearing anything like that."

He brushed across her clit, making her muscles flutter, her hips jerk forward. Katie's hand flew to his shoulder, using him as a brace to keep from swaying as her knees threatened to give out beneath her. Though he was hot everywhere else, his fingertips felt cool against her heated skin, and she hooked a foot through the back of a nearby chair, yanking it toward them. It enabled her to rest her sandal on it, spreading her legs further to allow Caleb room to explore.

"And here I thought you were one of those creative types who didn't need everything spelled out for him. I should've walked away the second I saw you tonight."

"There's still time to walk away," Caleb pointed out, sliding his fingers into her pussy. He curled his fingers against her walls, stroking her flesh as he jerked his wrist. "Just say the word."

The only word that came to Katie's mind at that minute was *more*. She didn't even realize she'd said it out loud until she heard him chuckle.

"Son of a bitch," she muttered. She yanked at his belt, pushing the zipper out of her way in order to find his throbbing length, the tip already wet with pre-come. Thank God they didn't have to worry about condoms. She'd long ago trusted Caleb to be straight with her about testing, and birth-control pills had been her best friend since she'd been in high school. "My life would be a hell of a lot simpler if I'd never met you."

Caleb laughed. "Oh, Katie, you don't mean that." He pulled his hand away from her and reached for his cock, his hand covering hers as he guided his head to her heat. He paused just before entering her. "Do you?"

The question took her by surprise. From the beginning, their relationship had been about sex, a carnal lust determined not to be dismissed when they were in each other's company. Certainly, they had fun together; Caleb was eloquent and charming with a direct wit that always made her laugh. And he was easy to work with, accepting decisions with little argument and possessing an uncanny eye for talent that drew crowds. But that was it. They never strayed to conversations that could in any way be construed as serious.

This query, however, broke that unspoken tenet.

Liquid eyes gazed at her in heavy-lidded expectation, and Katie felt her stomach clench. "Simpler doesn't mean better," she conceded. Bracing against the wall, she coiled her arms over his shoulders in order to pull his lips to hers. Their kiss left her breathless. "God, I've missed you."

"Missed you too," Caleb gasped as he finally pushed into her. He moved slowly, each thrust deliberate and torturous. She tried to push for something more, but he resisted all her efforts, as though he was taking her earlier warning very seriously.

His languorous pace was set to torture her, she was sure of it. He was forcing her to experience every thick inch of him, to feel how he stretched her, filled her, glanced over her g-spot as he slid inside. Katie's lips parted against his, swallowing his shallow breaths, and she clung to him until her clit ground against the base of his cock. Then she wrapped a long leg around his hips, refusing him the space to move, as she devoured his mouth in a kiss that made her head spin. If this was all she was going to get, she wanted to make it last. It would have to fuel fantasies for weeks to come.

Caleb snuck his hands under her, gripping her ass, and deepened the kiss. He kissed her like he wanted to feel every bit of her, wanted to fuck her and devour her and know every inch of her. Katie understood. She felt the same sort of hunger whenever they were together, and nobody could satisfy it like he could. She knew they didn't have much time up there—somebody could discover them at any moment—but she was sure he wasn't going to rush things. She loosened her leg around him, and he shocked her by pulling back as much as he could and slamming forward.

It drove the air from her lungs. Stifling her instinct to cry out, Katie brought her mouth back to his, losing herself in the waves of pleasure ricocheting from clit to tit and back again. She was going to come quickly, and she was likely to come more than once, but there was no way she could stop rocking with his forceful strokes, or squeezing around his thick shaft, or sweeping her tongue inside his mouth to taste every last inch of him.

"Fuck, I was so wrong," she muttered between kisses.

"Wrong about what?" he asked, his voice tight.

"When I saw you up here. Earlier. I thought..."

Another powerful thrust hit her clit in just the right way, and Katie clamped down around his cock as her orgasm burned through her in a fresh wave of fire. She had to wait until the quaking began to calm, until she'd sucked down enough air to speak again, to finish the thought.

"...I thought I didn't need to see you tonight, that it would be more trouble than it's worth." Her trembling mouth brushed over his. "I was wrong."

"I'm glad you changed your mind," Caleb murmured before deepening the kiss. He continued to thrust into her, but his body was taut and trembling against her sweaty skin, like he might shatter against her. "I won't be able to stay away from you."

His words made her smile, but she hid it from him by licking a path along his jaw, nibbling at his neck as she tugged his shirt up and out of her way. She wanted to feel his hard muscles, feel his slick skin sliding across hers, but that wouldn't be possible here at the Wooden Nickel or even at one of their places. That was inviting getting caught, and if she was going to have one last night with Caleb, she didn't want it tainted with worry.

Katie pulled back to meet his dark eyes. "How badly do you want this to continue tonight?"

The air whistled between Caleb's teeth as he inhaled sharply. "What do I have to do to show you how bad I want it?"

"Help me sneak into the executive bungalow. The bigwigs went back to the city instead of spending the night, so it's all empty and lonely until next weekend." She ran her tongue over her bottom lip. "And you have to stay naked with me the whole night to make up for lost time."

Anybody else might have balked at the suggestion of using the executive bungalow, but he didn't miss a beat. "Absolutely. Do you have the keys, or are we staging an old-fashioned breaking and entering?"

"That depends." She traced a flat nipple before flicking the hard tip with her fingernail. "You want to waste time waiting for me to go *all* the way back to my office to get the key, and then *all* the way out to the bungalow? Or do you want to get straight to having your wicked way with me on every flat surface we can find?"

Katie didn't know if it was her sinful promise, or the scrape of her finger across his nipple, but he shuddered against her, a low moan escaping his mouth as he thrust into her one final time, slamming against her clit. The sudden pressure sent sharp pleasure through her, and she curled her nails into his skin as her second orgasm overwhelmed her. He clamped his hand over her mouth as she opened it, muffling her shout of pleasure.

His breath was hot against her face as he silently gulped for air, his mouth so close to her cheek that it almost felt like he was kissing her. When he spoke, she could hear the smile in his voice. "I can get us in without a key."

She leaned into the caress, nuzzling against the rasp of his hair. "Of course you can," she whispered with a laugh. "You, Caleb Beckett, are a man of astonishing talents."

"Including several I intend to reacquaint you with tonight."

"Is that a promise?"

"Or a threat. But it's all the same in the end, isn't it?" Caleb said, finally disentangling himself. He zipped up his pants, but made no other effort to straighten his clothes or hide the fact that he had just fucked her against the wall.

Using the wall for support, Katie did her jeans back up, her eyes never leaving Caleb's. She wasn't sure what game he was playing at, but this entire encounter had already shattered every rule she'd ever given herself in regards to him. At least she was giving their affair the send-off it deserved. They had started with an explosive bang; it made sense that it end the same way.

Tomorrow.

"I think there's a door out there, waiting for you to break your way in," she teased. She ran her fingers along the lapel of his suit, then curled the fabric into her grasp in order to pull him flush again with her body. "Ready to go tear it down?"

"Tear it down?" He kissed the corner of her mouth. "I think you know I work with a bit more finesse than that."

She smiled and kissed him back. "I'm counting on it."

Chapter Two

The bungalow was set apart from the rest of the resort, so the higher-ups wouldn't be imposed on by the people who actually paid their salaries. Caleb had never been inside the executives' rooms, but he knew they would be about a hundred times nicer than his own modest residence. Somehow, that made the whole experience that much more gratifying.

He looked sideways at Katie while she waited impatiently for him to jimmy the lock. She looked like silver in the moonlight, and his fingers itched to touch her smooth skin again, or run through her soft hair. Just the sight of her was enough to make his groin tight. Sometimes, just a glimpse of her would set his blood pressure sky high as his heart jumped to double-time. To say that she was the most beautiful woman he had ever seen would almost be an understatement.

She thought this would be their last night together, but Caleb was not going to accept that. He understood her job was on the line. He would never ask her to sacrifice her job for him—that wasn't what their relationship was like. And besides, he knew how much this gig meant to her. She took it seriously, and she loved it—flourished under the responsibility. But this was not going to be their last night together.

The lock clicked. Straightening, he pushed the door open and bowed at the waist. "After you."

A dimple played in her cheek when she smiled. "I hope those manners aren't going to get in the way of our having fun later on," she teased as she swept past.

"I don't think that'll be a problem," Caleb said, kicking the door shut and reaching for her at the same time, wrapping his fingers around her wrist to yank her against his chest.

Before she could say a word, he worked her pants open for the second time that night. He couldn't be patient. He had been waiting nine months to get her alone again, and he thought about her every single night. He dropped to his knees, pulling her jeans down her legs, taking her sandals off at the same time. Her thong followed the pants, so he had a clear view of her glistening pussy. He inhaled deeply, heady from the smell of their sex at the club. Gently, he parted her lips, exposing her swollen clit to his tongue.

Katie tangled her fingers in his hair, guiding him closer as she propped her heel up on the wall behind her. When she tilted her head back as well, it made her long neck seem even longer, her slim body even more graceful. "Have I mentioned how much I like the new look?" she said. "I've been wondering all night what it would feel like if you ate me out. If it would feel different, or tickle, or something."

Caleb grinned, pleased that she'd noticed. He teased her clit with the tip of his tongue, his cheek brushing against her thigh. "Does it?"

"It feels..."

The words were choked off when he circled her sensitive clit again, then swept lower to do the same with her wet opening. While his fingers kept her spread, his thumbs stroked the satin flesh of her inner lips, keeping the same slow pace he knew would drive her crazy. Katie's fingers tightened, and the small pulls of his hair only made his cock throb that much harder.

"The only thing that could make this better…" She'd found her voice again, though it was rough with desire. "…would be if I had you in my mouth too."

Caleb moaned against her clit, and her flesh vibrated against his lips. Without diverting his attention from her, he unzipped his pants, freeing his hard cock. He could already feel her hot mouth wrapped around his shaft.

"I could do this all night," he said, looking at her from beneath his lashes. "Do you believe that I could suck your clit"—he demonstrated by pulling her clit between his teeth— "all night?" He swept his tongue along her lips. "I could lick you, taste every inch of you." He moved his tongue over her again, lapping up her juices. "I could fuck you with my tongue all night." Now he slid his tongue into her passage, his fingers tightening on her thighs, holding her firmly against his face.

"I believe you," Katie breathed. "God, do I believe you."

For a moment, she undulated against his mouth, riding his tongue as assuredly as if it was his cock. Then her knee straightened, and Katie placed the foot she'd had against the wall onto his shoulder. With a strength that always took him by surprise, she forced Caleb to loosen his hold on her thighs, breaking the seal of his lips from her glistening pussy. She smiled down at him as she pushed him back onto the floor.

"Tell me you want me to suck you," she ordered without removing her foot.

A shiver raced down Caleb's spine, and his cock jerked. He watched her with half-closed eyes, unable to look away. He couldn't resist reaching up to drag his thumb over her swollen clit. "I want you to suck my cock, Kate."

Pure hunger gleamed in her blue eyes. Without looking away, Katie grabbed the hem of her camisole and pulled it off over her head, leaving her completely naked for his pleasure. "I don't want to miss feeling you against any inch of me," she said, right before sinking to her knees at his side.

She made short work of his clothes, stripping him almost faster than he'd done her. By the time she was done, his hands were itching to grab her and drag her back to his mouth, but Katie didn't seem quite ready for that. She ran long, elegant fingers along his cock, circling his balls once and then sliding back up its length. Only then did she bend over, her pale blonde hair trailing across the darker skin of his stomach as she let her tongue take the same path as her hand.

"Oh...Katie...God..." Caleb sighed, relaxing against the floor.

For the moment, he couldn't do anything except close his eyes and give in to the overwhelming pleasure. Nobody knew how to do what she could do. He licked his lips, and the taste of her that lingered there sent another wave of pleasure through him, prompting him to reach for her. He curled his fingers around her thigh and pulled her leg across his chest, coaxing her until her pussy was just inches from his face. She never broke contact with his cock, her lips so soft against his skin, her tongue so clever. He waited until she swallowed his shaft, then gripped her hips and brought her swollen flesh to his waiting mouth.

The first contact of his tongue against her clit made her moan, a long, drawn-out sound that reverberated through his cock. The second drove her nails into the sensitive skin of his inner thigh, scraping across his sac at the same time, while the third got her moving up his length, catching at the head in order to swirl her tongue around the crown at the tempo he was setting.

Caleb focused on her clit, lapping her flesh until it throbbed against his lips. Her hips jerked with each swipe of his tongue, driving her clit against his teeth. He struggled to concentrate, but it was difficult with her mouth searing him, her breath tickling his skin each time she exhaled. He sucked her clit between his teeth, biting gently as he teased the tip with his tongue. She slammed her hips down, and retaliated by scraping her teeth along his shaft.

Katie didn't do anything by halves. Whether it was work or pleasure, she threw everything she had into it with an energy that belied her calm exterior. It was one of the things that had first drawn Caleb to her. The potential of unlocking her passion had been too powerful to resist, and he hadn't been disappointed. Even three years later, she still surprised him on a nightly basis.

Her orgasms were no exception.

While her body quivered in violent throes, her mouth and hands never ceased their assaults on his flesh. Her fingers forced his thighs apart, shaking as they smoothed down beneath his ass and pulled him even deeper into her throat. The sounds she could never stifle when she came echoed into his cock, and the ragged sensations left by her teeth sharpened to fiery peaks.

Caleb dug his fingers into her flesh, holding her against him, intent on catching every bit of her juices as she came. His hips jerked erratically, unable to find a steady rhythm. His entire body was shaking, pushing for more, always seeking out more of her. He slid his tongue down her flesh to thrust into her slick, clenching passage, triggering another orgasm. As she cried out again, his balls tightened, and he exploded deep in her mouth. She didn't lift her head or pull away—she never did—until he was completely spent.

Her tongue traced upward along his softening shaft, her breath satin warm against his skin. "We're going to have to wait here for a minute, I think." With her long-legged grace that whispered wicked promises for later, Katie peeled their sweaty bodies apart to turn around and curl into his side, her head propped up in her hand so that the ends of her pale hair tickled along his shoulder. Her smile was slow and satisfied. "Walking might be asking a little much right now."

"Yeah, a little downtime might be a good idea," Caleb agreed, the bottoms of his feet still tingling. He skimmed his hand over her shoulder and down her arm, entwining his fingers with hers. "Do you regret leaving the bar with me yet?"

"No," she replied without pause. Then her lashes ducked as she glanced down at their hands. "Though I regret we're only going to have tonight."

Caleb knew that even though she had given in to him this time, she wouldn't change her mind about their future prospects. Not unless something changed. Without releasing her fingers, he brought her hand to his mouth. "If this is all we have, we better make it memorable. Don't you think?"

Her clear gaze followed the path of their hands, her swollen mouth curving into a smile when his tongue traced the outline of her fingers. "I think that's the best suggestion I've heard all week."

Caleb slid his leg between her thighs and freed her hand so he could wrap his arm around her. "Then we'll get on that as soon as we can walk to the bed. In the meantime, I've got to know. How do you propose we stay away from each other for the next three months? It's going to be a very long summer."

Her nose wrinkled in a moue of distaste. "Oh, sure. Ask the tough questions after you've already put my brain in reverse."

"I know, it's hardly fair. But clearly, you don't want to give this...us...up any more than I do." He looked down, tracing the curve of her body with his eyes. "I missed you, you know."

Katie took longer to respond this time. "I missed you too," she murmured. "You have no idea how much I was looking forward to this summer when Quentin sprang his little ultimatum on me."

Caleb thought he might have some idea. It was getting harder to leave her every year, and Labor Day had quickly become his most hated non-holiday. The day after Labor Day always dawned with him going south, and her going north, with only the promise of the next summer between them.

"It must have come as quite the shock. Though I suppose we're lucky he didn't fire us both as soon as he found out."

"He's too smart to lose you. He knows what a huge asset you are to Jubilee."

Caleb snorted. "It's not me he's worried about losing, sweetheart."

"He doesn't want to lose *either* of us," Katie insisted. "But that doesn't mean he won't replace us if he has to."

Caleb had his doubts that Quentin would carry through with his threat of firing Katie. She was the best thing that had ever happened to this dump, and everybody knew it. He did know a way to fix things, but he didn't want to go that far yet. Not until he knew how Katie felt about him—if this was more than just sex for her. "Do you already have plans for September fourth? Quentin didn't say anything about seeing each other on our own time, did he?"

In the circle of his arm, Katie stiffened, but when she pulled away to look at him, it was genuine surprise that lit her eyes. "No, to both questions, but...you always go back to Miami when the season's over."

"I do," Caleb agreed. "But I don't have any commitments until the beginning of October, and it recently occurred to me that I haven't seen as much of Beantown as I'd like."

The smile that began to blossom on her face was hesitant, but her voice betrayed a hidden excitement. "I didn't think you'd want to. I mean, if you want to come up, I've got more than enough time accrued to take September off. We could have a real vacation for a change."

Caleb matched her smile and kissed her. The kiss was unlike any other they'd shared that night. He coaxed her lips apart, pushing his tongue in to taste the salty-sweetness of her mouth. Holding her against him, he gradually deepened the caress, until there was nothing in his world except her soft mouth, and his cock began to stir again. When he finally pulled back, she was staring at him with wide eyes. "I think we should try to make it to the bed now."

৪০৪০৪০

It was the dread of the approaching dawn that drew Katie awake. After hours of touching and exploring and enjoying, time made up for months of absence from each other, she had fallen asleep with Caleb spooned behind her, his arm tight around her waist, his face buried in her hair. Only nights with him were capable of knocking her out so completely, but as always, in the back of her mind, there was that little voice, ready to remind her that they couldn't get caught, that she couldn't risk sleeping the night away and getting exposed sneaking away from his place. This wasn't the same set-up, and they didn't officially have to be in to work that morning, but housekeeping would still come around the bungalow to ensure that everything was all right with it as part of their rounds. Katie wasn't willing to risk their jobs over a couple hours of sleep.

When she rolled over to wake Caleb up, however, she found his side of the bed empty. His clothes were still on the chair where they'd dumped them, and the door stood ajar, but when she strained to hear what he might be doing, silence was the only sound that greeted her. Pushing back the blankets, she rose and walked out to the dark living room. He wasn't there either. Katie was about to call out his name when she saw the blinds leading to the patio had been pushed aside.

He must have gone outside for some fresh air, she realized. A quick glance at the clock on the DVD player told her she had at least an hour until sunrise. There was plenty of time for her to join him.

She only took a single step. This was going to be their last night together until September. Though they hadn't discussed it further, Katie knew that Caleb would follow through on his plan to come up to Boston after the Jubilee season was over, but that still left three very long months ahead of them to try and endure without indulging their desires. She wanted to give him something now to make the wait worth it. Something special.

She knew exactly what to do.

It took very little time to get ready. Only five minutes elapsed from the time Katie made her decision to the time she slid open the patio door.

Caleb stood at the railing, casually smoking a cigarette as he leaned against the half-wall and gazed out at the dark ocean. He hadn't bothered to get dressed, and even in the dim light spilling from the bungalow, she saw the outline of his muscled back tapering down to his slim hips. Her mouth watered. God, he was gorgeous. Even now, with her plan firmly in mind, she just wanted to walk up to him, sink to her knees and worship him with her tongue. It took everything she had to simply stand there.

The sound of the door made him glance back. Her appearance kept him from looking away.

Without her own wardrobe, Katie had had to improvise. She wore Caleb's suit jacket with nothing underneath, his belt cinched at her waist to turn it into the tiniest of dresses. Her hair was swept up using pencils from the desk in order to pin it in place, and she'd slicked on a fresh coat of lip gloss to make her mouth shine. Her high-heeled sandals finished the ensemble.

"You left me all alone in bed," she scolded.

"I thought you deserved to sleep. You had a long night." He was staring at her like he had never seen her before. "You look like you're ready to go dancing again."

"I was thinking...something a little more private."

With long, slow strides, Katie closed the distance between them, plucking the cigarette from his fingers and taking a deep drag on it before stubbing it out on the nearby ashtray. The nicotine sent a quick buzz to her head, making it spin, but she didn't let it stop her from taking Caleb by the hand and leading him to one of the deck chairs.

"Three months is a very long time," she said as she pushed him gently into the seat.

"It's an eternity," Caleb said, reaching out to push the jacket aside. She playfully slapped his hand away. "Are you going to do something to make the wait more tolerable?"

"Something like that." She circled the chair, dragging her fingertips along his collarbone until she stood behind him. Then she slid her hand down his chest and caressed the flat of his stomach as she leaned in to murmur into his ear. "I know how tough it's going to be this summer. Wanting to touch you, but not being able to. Falling asleep all hot and sweaty even though the AC is cranked as high as it'll go. Nobody's ever made me feel like you do, Caleb. Nobody."

She smiled as his cock jerked, and he arched his back slightly, pushing against her hand. His voice was thick when he spoke, like something was blocking his throat. "That sounds like hell, Katie."

"Which is why I want to make it up to you now." She skimmed her mouth along his shoulder before straightening and finishing the circuit around the chair. Standing in front of him, Katie toyed with the ends of the belt. Though she knew she appeared calm and in control to Caleb, her heart was thumping like a jackhammer at what she was about to suggest. "Do you still have that fantasy about bending me over your knee? Because I think some of my bad behavior the past few weeks might just merit some of your...*personal* attention."

Caleb's eyes widened, and it was impossible to ignore his physical reaction. "What...what bad behavior would that be?"

She lifted a shoulder in a nonchalant half-shrug. "Ignoring you, for starters." She placed her foot on the arm of the chair so that her pussy was just visible to him. "And I gave you the brush-off at the Nickel tonight. Some men might take that as a personal affront."

"Some men might," Caleb agreed, reaching out to slide his fingers up her thigh. "I wasn't personally offended myself." He flashed a smile at her. "I knew you wouldn't ignore me for long."

In spite of the welcome soreness from their night of fucking, the feather glances of his fingertips made her breath hitch. Maybe giving into his fantasy of control wouldn't be nearly as hard as she thought.

"Then there's the whole caving to Quentin thing." It shocked her how even her voice was. The rest of her was anything but. "Don't tell me that doesn't piss you off, even a little bit."

His eyes sparked and his mouth curved, a sign that he knew the game, before his face hardened. "I have to admit, I expected better of you, Katie. Since when have you let anybody tell you what to do?"

"I know, I know. But it's too late to do anything about it now. Except for telling you."

She dropped her foot to his bare thigh, running her toes along the taut muscle before putting it back to the ground. Quelling the uncertainty flaring inside her, Katie sat in Caleb's lap, making sure to trap his hard cock between her thighs as she leaned back against his chest.

"I should have told you sooner," she confessed. Her hands went to the belt, undoing the buckle. Slowly, she pulled the strap free from her waist, feeling it slide between their bodies in a long, delicious stroke. His cock jumped against her pussy. She could only assume it was from the sensations of the leather burning across his skin. "But I was afraid of how you'd react."

Caleb gripped her wrist with one hand and took the belt from her fingers with the other. "I have to say, I'm more disappointed than angry." He wrapped the leather around one of her wrists. "Clasp your fingers together. Yeah, like that." The leather went around her second wrist. His breath tickled her ear as he cinched the belt tighter, lashing her hands together.

This was new. In all the time they'd been together, not once had Katie let Caleb bind her in any way. It left her feeling too vulnerable, too out of control, and she'd begged off the few times he'd brought it up. He'd been his usual gracious self and backed off the subject, but she always knew that the desire was there. That, and the spanking fantasy. He'd whispered that one in her ear one night the previous summer while she'd been riding him, caressing her ass as he described in that electric voice what he wanted to do to it. Though she'd nixed the idea afterward, it didn't change the fact that she'd come so hard that time that she was out for the rest of the night.

She was equal parts excited and terrified about what was going to happen. What had convinced her in the end that she could do this was knowing she could trust him.

Without the belt to keep it closed, the jacket fell open, baring Katie's breasts to the warm predawn air. "What are you going to do?" she asked, keeping her voice small.

He kissed the back of her neck, his moustache tickling her. "I'm going to show you how disappointed I am," he murmured, hot lips brushing against her cool skin. "And I'm going to make sure you don't forget." He paused for a moment, before kissing a path to her ear. When he spoke, his tone was different, his words soft. "If you want to stop, just say patio."

Though her throat was dry, Katie whispered her assent. Caleb might be the one issuing commands at the moment, but his concern for a safe word was all she needed to surrender the last of her worries. He wouldn't hurt her. Except in the best way possible.

Caleb lifted her from his lap and turned her over, positioning her across his thighs. He pushed her jacket up, exposing her ass to the early morning air and to his hand. She braced herself, but he surprised her by running his palm over the curve of her cheek, caressing her lightly. Then, without warning, he brought the flat of his palm down over her flesh.

The sudden sting made her jerk against his legs. One of the pencils tumbled from her hair, letting a long strand escape to drape over her shoulder, but all Katie felt was the burn already fading along her ass. That wasn't so bad, she thought, but then his body moved against her side, and his hand struck again, this time finding a fresh patch of skin to enflame.

His cock was hard and slick with pre-come against her stomach, and it twitched against her every time he brought his hand down. "What are you going to tell Quentin the next time you see him?"

Caleb expected her to be coherent enough to respond to questions? Shivers ran through her with every heated stroke, racing along nerve endings already too sensitive for more, and small whimpers accompanied the squirms of her body as she rubbed against his hard lines. He caressed the burn after each blow, but that only served to heighten the sensations the next time his palm made contact. It took two more for her to remember that he'd asked her something, and another to find the breath to answer.

"What...what do you...?" Katie cried out as one slap stung a little bit more than its predecessors, and her back bowed away from his legs for endless seconds before she could relax again. She realized Caleb was hesitating, but though she knew he probably anticipated the safe word to come any moment, she refused to take this away from him.

She swallowed hard and tried again. "I'll tell him whatever you want me to tell him," she whispered. On a whim, she added, "Sir."

"Tell him...tell him that you're going to see whoever you want, and do whatever you like. If he doesn't like it, you tell him he can fuck off." His hand came down then, emphasizing his point. His fingers curled against her heated skin, and his tone dropped to something dark and silky. "Do you understand?"

Her wrists strained against the belt binding them together, but Katie kept them down and out of the way as she risked a glance back. Caleb's eyes were black and fathomless in the indistinct light, resting on her in expectation, and something in her chest tightened. Supposedly, this was just a game, this was about Caleb's fantasy and not real life, and maybe she wouldn't use the exact words he chose for her, but right then, Katie thought she could do it. She could talk to Quentin. Not once had their work suffered in all the time they'd been together, and if it took Quentin three years to find out the secret, then obviously they were doing something right.

"Yes, sir," she breathed. "I understand perfectly."

"Good." The word seemed to vibrate through her body. He slipped his hand between her thighs, his fingers gliding against her wet pussy. He caressed her flesh for a moment before sliding two fingers inside of her. "I'm a fair man. If you do that, you'll be rewarded."

She had known that she'd been aroused, even through the pain. She still wasn't quite prepared for how wet she sounded, or how her muscles clamped down around his fingers, or how badly she craved more. It felt like she would fly apart if he stopped touching her, and Katie was prepared to do whatever it took to make sure that didn't happen.

"Pocket," she panted. His sharp intake of breath alarmed her, and she realized that the single word was far too close to their safe one for her not to make clear. "In the coat pocket," she said, this time more clearly enunciating "I brought something else out."

Without removing his hand from her pussy, Caleb reached across her body to root around and extract the small tube of Vaseline she'd stuck in there. Though he frowned slightly in confusion, she tossed her hair and gave him a teasing smile. "It's not exactly K-Y, but I thought it would do in a pinch."

"You're a woman of many surprises," Caleb said with real appreciation in his voice. She couldn't stop her whimper as he removed his fingers from her. She watched as he smeared the Vaseline on the two fingers still wet from her juices. He slid one fingertip between her cheeks, pushing his first knuckle past the tight ring of muscle.

Katie tensed. She knew what was going to happen, had planned for this very thing, but that didn't stop her body from reacting to the intrusion. Anal play had never interested her, and while she understood other women got off on it as much as regular fucking, it was a step she'd never taken, not even with Caleb. The subject hadn't even been brought up since that first wild weekend they'd spent together. He'd learned her boundaries, and he'd respected them all this time.

But now it was time for those boundaries to be stretched. If she could handle some spanking—even get excited by it—then she could do this. For both of them.

Caleb pushed his finger in slowly, up to his third knuckle, and paused. He ran his other hand down her spine, a light, soothing motion, but it didn't distract her from what he was doing. He seemed to sense when she was finally comfortable with the intrusion, because it was only then that he moved out of her. He paused for a moment as she relaxed against him before repeating it, this time with two slick fingers.

Her throat worked until she found her voice again. "Are you still disappointed?"

Caleb didn't answer immediately. He jerked his wrist, pulling his hand away, and then thrusting into her once again. He set a slow, deliberate pace. "No," he said, as she writhed against his hand. "No, not at all."

"Good." The unfamiliar discomfort faded with every stroke of his fingers, to be replaced by an ache that Katie recognized all too well. Her hips began to pump to meet his hand, and her nipples scraped across his thighs. Every movement meant his cock rubbed along her already slick stomach, and soon, his soft sighs joined her louder moans.

Katie felt the tension in his body. His muscles were tight, and each sigh turned into a ragged breath. When he pulled his hand away from her, she expected him to flip her around and end his torment. Instead, he coated a third finger, and thrust all three into her stretched flesh. "Are you ready, Katie?"

"You know I am." She twisted her neck to look back at him, and her eyes burned as much as her ass did. "God, Caleb, just fuck me already. Please. This is driving me crazy."

Caleb moved quickly, lifting her off his lap to her feet. He covered his cock with the Vaseline, stroking his shaft to coat every inch of himself. She settled on his lap again, her back against his chest. She stared out across the ocean as he pulled the head of his cock along her ass, then pushed it past her puckered flesh.

Everything stopped. All she felt was the insistent pressure as Caleb sank into her body, slow and slick, stretching her far beyond what his fingers had. He didn't stop and start to allow her to adjust, but neither did he force himself, keeping his pace patient and unhurried for long seconds. It seared, inside and out, until Katie was convinced her skin would ignite at the slightest provocation.

When he was completely sheathed, Caleb coiled his arm around her waist, pulling her even closer to his chest. His breath was hot where he dropped gentle kisses along her shoulder, and it spurred her to finally exhale, a long, shuddering sound that wracked her body.

The waves crashing against the beach echoed the crashing in her ears. The belt's long tail brushed against her knees until he grabbed it and yanked it back, pulling her arms tight against her torso. She tilted her head back to look at him, but he caught her chin and forced her head forward again. It felt like every inch of his body was touching every inch of hers, and his breath and lips and words were so warm against her skin. She couldn't hear everything he said, but she caught the occasional *so good,* and *so beautiful,* and *so tight.*

His thrusts were shallow at first, but gradually became longer, deeper, until he was lifting her almost completely off his lap before dragging her back down again. Katie wished desperately that she could see him, or that he could see her, but Caleb was unyielding in this, his hands joining in his mouth's assault. Calloused fingertips dug into her soft inner thighs, spreading her wider. She was begging long before she even thought not to.

"Don't...don't stop, don't...please, Caleb, just...just, I need you to..."

Caleb shuddered. "I won't. Oh God, Kate..." Each stroke seemed longer, slower, more intense than the one before it. "I've thought about this so many times." His words were pulled from him, like the effort to speak was almost enough to undo him.

Coherent thought seemed impossible, but still, the question demanded to be heard. "Why didn't you ask me?" Though he wouldn't allow her to look back at him, it didn't stop Katie from leaning her head back against his shoulder, tendrils of her hair slipping over his skin as she stared up at the starless sky. "I would do almost anything for you."

Several seconds passed in silence, and Katie wondered if Caleb even heard her at all. When he finally spoke, there was something heavy in his voice, the breathy pleasure completely gone. He sheathed himself completely, his hold on her firm, and said, "I know, Katie."

Part of her was tempted to use the safe word. She didn't want to play this game where she couldn't even look at him. But she didn't. Katie feared that if she uttered it aloud, Caleb would stop entirely, and that was the last thing she wanted to happen.

So she closed her eyes and called his image before her mind's eye instead. It was simple with his hands growing bolder, his mouth hungrier. Teeth scraped against her neck, and one of his hands strayed from her thigh to trace her outer lips. And when a finger flicked across her clit, seemingly as if by accident, it sent her crashing over the edge, her entire body undulating against his cock, his chest, his strong legs, as her orgasm swept through her.

"Oh...Katie...Katie..." She felt him tense behind her before his climax shook his frame. Every muscle seemed to tremble, his chest seized, and his cock twitched and jerked against her tight walls. "God...God..." He panted, thrusting into her one final time before collapsing back against his chair, holding her with one arm wrapped around her waist.

The sun crested in front of them, warming her skin and turning the gray water golden. Despite the beauty of the sunrise, and her own deep satisfaction, a sadness washed over her. This was it, for three months.

"Katie? I meant to tell you something earlier tonight."

She squeezed her eyes shut. If he tried to convince her to let the affair continue behind Quentin's back anyway, she didn't know how she'd be able to say no. "Didn't Rosaria get you a slot on the agenda for Monday's meeting?" she joked.

"I won't be at the staff meeting on Monday. I'm handing in my resignation. I know it's short notice, but Lenny should be able to pick up the slack. He's been angling for my job for the last two seasons, anyway."

His words were a blast of cold water over her satiated limbs. Twisting out of his arms, Katie swung around to stare at him in disbelief. "You're quitting? Why? You can't. I need you."

"I need you too, Katie. This winter was the winter from hell. I got through it because I was thinking about you. I just wanted to see you again. And now I find out I can't even touch you for three months? I can't treat you like the woman I love?" He shook his head. "No. This job is not worth that. Quentin pays me for my time, that doesn't mean he gets to dictate my life."

She didn't even hear the last of his statements. Her brain was still stuck on what he'd said in the middle.

"The woman you...*what?*"

"Love. I love you." He offered an easy smile. "Enough to see if we've got something more than sex here."

Katie felt like she'd been thrown overboard without a life jacket. In all the time they'd spent together, they'd never talked about feelings. It was about fun, and sex, and having a good time, and more sex, and why in hell was Caleb changing the rules on her now? What was wrong with what they'd had? Except they couldn't have that any more because of Quentin's little ultimatum. If Caleb asked her again how she planned on getting through the summer without touching each other, Katie still didn't have a clue how she'd answer. She just didn't know.

What she did know was that she'd never been with anybody like Caleb before. It wasn't just the physical, though that was pretty amazing. It was how talented he was, how easygoing, how certain of his own abilities without having the need to flaunt it in anybody else's face. She enjoyed his company, and frankly, the past three summers with Jubilee had been the best of her professional career. He made her better, damn it, and now he wanted to change all that? For what?

For love. He loved her.

"What do you think is going to happen?" she asked carefully. "We've never even had an official date. You might decide that I'm a real bitch when we're out in the open, and then where will you be?"

His smile never wavered. "That's a chance I'm willing to take, though I know you better than that." He leaned forward, his eyes earnest. "I'm giving you the option, Kate. I don't want you to put your career in jeopardy. You've got a real future with Jubilee. You make this place what it is, and I can see how happy it makes you. But I think you could be my future...if you'll have me."

The sincerity of his words made her heart pound. Katie didn't think of her future in terms of men or relationships; it had always been about the job, about what she needed to do next in order to get the new promotion.

But even as she thought that, she realized it wasn't entirely true. How many times last winter had she spent an evening dreaming of what it would be like to see Caleb again? And she could remember at least three different dates where she'd sat there, comparing the man with her to Caleb. She'd missed him, and she'd anticipated spending four glorious months together. She'd made plans for them, all the way up to Quentin's ultimatum. There was no way around it; she considered him a part of her future. Now here he was, offering her even more.

Katie held up her wrists, still bound in his belt. "Undo me, please."

Caleb slowly unbuckled the belt and slid the leather over her wrists. He dropped the belt to the ground without taking his eyes from her. "Thank you."

Though her pulse was racing, her voice was deceptively soft. "For what?"

"For trusting me enough to let go."

She smiled. "You make that incredibly easy." Her hands were stiff from having been in one position for so long, but Katie stretched them out along his bare chest, her gaze dropping to watch her fingers stroke his still damp skin. "I've never considered my...feelings for you," she confessed. "I'm much better organizing people than I am at compartmentalizing my emotions."

He covered her hands with his, pressing them against his skin. "I know. I don't expect you to declare your love for me right now or anything, Katie. But I do hope you'd be willing to consider your feelings now."

She *was* willing. But it was still way too fast for her. She needed time to sort it all through in her head. "You're singing at the launch next week, right?" His nod was hesitant, but the confirmation was all Katie wanted. "Don't quit yet. Give me a week. To think about all this. And I'd like for you to be my date at the afterparty."

"Katie, I..." Caleb paused and nodded. "You know I'll be there."

"With me, though." She smoothed her palms over his shoulders so that her breasts were crushed to his chest and their mouths were separated by a hair's breadth. "I want everyone to see that I'm with the hottest man in the room."

Caleb smashed his mouth against hers, kissing her until she was breathless. "I'll be with you. Anywhere you want to go."

All Katie did was smile before losing herself in another of his heart-stopping kisses. Maybe she didn't need so much time after all.

Chapter Three

Caleb felt the music long after the gig was over. The bass thrumming through the ground, vibrating through his feet, the drums following the rhythm of his heart, and the howling guitar tying everything together. He felt the energy of the crowd long after he left the stage. There was nothing like that energy, and nothing left him as drained, or as satisfied. They danced, they sang, they shouted, they sweated, and he took it all, draining it from them like a vampire.

But tonight was different. The only person he felt was Katie. The bright lights in his eyes obscured his vision, but it didn't matter. He knew exactly where she was standing all night, and his eyes were drawn to her lithe figure again and again. He didn't allow himself to be distracted from the music, but for the first time he was eager to finish the gig and willing to leap off the stage as soon as the music ended.

Despite that, he didn't get a chance to see her until the party. She was waiting for him near the door where they arranged to meet, holding an ice-cold bottle of water and a towel. He took them both gratefully, wiping the sweat from his face before wrapping his arm around her waist and pulling her into an embrace.

"Did you like the show?"

"Loved it." Her halter-style sundress left her arms bare, and without even a glance at the crowd around her, Katie lifted them to drape over his shoulders. "You had them eating out of the palm of your hand."

"Really?" He kissed her softly, holding himself back from what he really wanted to do. That could wait until they weren't surrounded by people. "What about you?"

Her eyes twinkled from some unknown delight. "You don't need to be onstage for me to want to eat you up." Abruptly, she twisted away, grabbing his free hand and lacing her fingers through his. "Come on. Everybody's here already. Let's mingle."

Caleb followed obediently, though he wasn't interested in mingling. He was very interested in the way her dress clung to her curves in just the right way. "Everybody? Who are you in such a hurry to see?"

Her shrug was playful. "Oh, if I had my way, we wouldn't be here at all. But the boss has got to put in an appearance, you know."

It struck him as she stopped and started amid the throng that he'd never seen her so relaxed in a work setting before. Usually, when they interacted professionally, Katie made sure to keep her distance from him, polite and friendly but slightly aloof so that the wrong assumption—or the right one, in their case—wouldn't be made. This new approach gave him hope that she was willing show their co-workers the woman he knew her to be behind closed doors. All the way until he spotted Quentin speaking with Lenny.

Caleb took her elbow, pulling her against his chest so he could speak in her ear. "You haven't told Quentin that I quit, have you?" It was a rhetorical question. He knew the answer. "What are you doing, Katie?"

Her smile faded a little. "What I do best. Organizing people." She pulled back, trying to lead him toward Quentin, but when he resisted, she squeezed his hand. "Trust me, Caleb."

Caleb wasn't worried about confronting Quentin, but he didn't feel he had anything to lose. Katie had something to lose. But she was a big girl, and he did trust her. How could he not? Every season, he watched her manage one of the largest resorts on the east coast with an ease that was almost intimidating. "I guess a party isn't a party without at least one awkward conversation. Lead on."

Quentin's smile was engaging as they approached. When he saw their clasped hands, however, his welcome visibly deflated. "I thought we'd discussed this, Katherine," he said after greetings had been exchanged.

"We did."

"And? Why are you throwing your career away like this? You can't tell me he's worth sacrificing your future for."

"Actually, he *is* worth it. But I'm not sacrificing anything." She shifted to Caleb. "Tell Quentin what you told me last weekend."

Caleb looked from Katie, to Quentin, and back again. She smiled encouragingly. Caleb had to admit, this would be a bit more satisfying than simply dropping a letter of resignation in the mail. "Oh, right." He smiled broadly. "I quit."

"But...but..." For an executive, Quentin wasn't exactly graceful in dealing with surprises. Probably why he'd responded so harshly with Katie in the first place. "He sang tonight. At a Jubilee launch. That puts him on the payroll."

"Yes," Katie agreed. "But not ours." Her gaze was steady as she turned back to Quentin, and she stood tall, every inch the manager Caleb knew her to be. "Caleb Beckett is too valuable a commodity for us to lose. The guests love him, he has an uncanny knack for nosing out talent, and if I let him walk away, I'd be slitting our throat for the summer. And don't try and tell me I'm biased. I tracked all the numbers for the past three years. Weekends he performs yield over double our regular grosses."

"That doesn't change the fact that he quit. And you still let him perform tonight."

"He *tried* to quit. I asked him to give me a week."

"To do what?"

Katie took a deep breath, glancing at Caleb out of the corner of her eye. "To split up his job. I've given Lenny all the administrative responsibility, the parts Caleb hates anyway, and Caleb is going to be responsible for the more creative aspects."

She launched into a detailed analysis of the talent agency she'd contracted with, but most of it was a blur to Caleb. The only part he caught for sure was that she'd signed over his employment agreement to this other company.

Quentin was frowning by the time she finished. "Maybe we're not signing his paycheck," he said, "but that doesn't mean we're not still the source of his income. You're subverting company policy for your own satisfaction, Katherine."

"You're right. I am. But company policy prohibits fellow employees from fraternizing, and technically, he doesn't work for me any more." Her gaze was unflinching. "I've dotted all the i's and crossed the t's, Quentin. Everything is aboveboard. But if you fight me on this, you lose both of us."

Caleb could only stare at her. If he didn't admire the hell out of her already, he did now. He never had a single doubt about his feelings for her, and now he knew she was *the one*, and he was one lucky bastard for finding her. He risked a glance at Quentin and managed not to laugh at the rainbow of colors on his face. Lenny was beaming, clearly pleased with the entire situation—no doubt his new duties came with a better paycheck as well.

"Well?" Caleb said, looking to Quentin. "This works for me if it works for you."

He could see the struggle in Quentin's eyes—pride versus greed. The man didn't like to be shown up, but he also didn't like to lose money. And holding out to save his pride would result in a great deal of revenue loss. They all knew it, perhaps Katie most of all.

"Fine. But don't think I won't have my lawyers look over all the contracts."

Katie smiled. "I wouldn't expect anything less." She stepped closer to Caleb, curling into his side. "Now if you'll excuse us, I'd like to finish basking in my boyfriend's fantastic opening night before I whisk him away. Enjoy the party."

Caleb was more than happy to steer her away from Quentin and back to the crowd, allowing the group to swallow them. His groin was uncomfortably tight, and his skin was warm, and his chest had bands around it. This was about more than just keeping his job—a job he was willing to walk away from. This proved she was willing to fight for him. This proved that maybe he wasn't the only one who needed this relationship.

"How long do we have to stay here?"

She paused from where they'd been heading for Rosaria. When she tilted her head to look at him, there was a flushed sheen high in her cheeks, and her eyes were impossibly bright. "Long enough for people to know that we're together. I'm done pretending you're not important to me."

Caleb folded her against his body, running his hands down her back to fit her against him. He rotated his hips once, grinding his erection against her thigh. "I'm a little concerned if we stay too long, everybody will get a demonstration of just how together we are."

Her smile turned sly. "And you have a problem with exhibitionism since *when?*"

"Oh, you know how shy I can be," he teased. The music shifted from background sound to something throbbing, meant to get people out on the floor. "Can I have this dance?"

Instead of answering right away, Katie slipped her arm around his neck to pull him into a hungry, lingering kiss that left his lips tingling and his cock aching. "I'll be with you," she said against his mouth. "Anywhere you want to go."

Caleb caught his breath, her words echoing in his mind, sending chills down his spine. "You're the most amazing woman I have ever met, Katherine Mayes." He began walking backwards, away from the dance floor and towards the back exit. "And I'm going to take you somewhere private right now and show you how much I love you."

She matched his pace, her smile never wavering. "Oh, sure, I get the hurdles clear for us to be together in public whenever we want, and the first thing you do is drag me back to your place."

"Only because it turns me on when you clear hurdles." They reached the door and he kicked it open, pulling her out behind him. "Let's make a date for a public appearance tomorrow night," he murmured as he pinned her against the wall. He didn't wait for her consent before claiming her mouth with a kiss that demonstrated exactly how much he wanted her.

Katie was breathless by the time Caleb broke away. "This probably sounds way too eighties teen movie, but this is going to be the best summer ever."

Caleb smiled. "Summer, winter, doesn't matter. Now that it's you and me, it's all going to be the best."

About the Author

Jamie Craig is the sum of two wholes: erotica writers Pepper Espinoza and Vivien Dean. Pepper has been writing since she was a child, but began her professional writing career in 2005 and now writes full time as well as attending graduate school and working toward a Masters in British and American Literature. A former resident of Los Angeles, she now lives in Utah. Vivien, the daughter of an author and sportswriter, also began writing at an early age, but eventually explored storytelling through acting and film production before coming back to prose. Vivien, her British husband and two children live in Northern California.

To learn more about Jamie Craig, please visit www.jamie-craig.com. Send an email to Jamie at jamie@jamie-craig.com

Look for these titles by
Jamie Craig

Now Available:

Craving Kismet
Trinity Broken

Second Wind

Dee S. Knight

Dedication

Pat, what would I do without you? For sure, there'd be no Second Wind—the ms would be sitting on a shelf. Always love and thanks to Vanessa, Skully, Jenn, Chris, Amy and Terri. You all are a godsend. And Jack, you give a second wind to my whole life. Thanks for being my hero.

Chapter One

"Cathy, don't, babe." The plaintive note in Rafe's voice almost stopped her, almost made Cathy Walker take her suitcase stuffed with nearly everything she owned back out of the car.

Almost.

"You're not being fair, Rafe. You know using that tone curls my toes and your little-boy look turns me to mush." She slammed the trunk lid and turned to face her husband. "But I won't be swayed this time. You have to make up your mind what you want. When you do, I'll make up my mind if I can live with your decision."

"What I want? I want you to be happy, God knows I do." He lowered his head and rubbed the back of his neck until she thought he might not leave any skin. "It's just..."

"You knew I wanted to work, you've known all along that's what I planned." She flung her arm out toward the wide-open spaces that represented their ranch. Correction, *Rafe's* ranch. "We *need* me to work. Yet you make me feel guilty for every minute I give to my job."

He looked up, his eyes ignited with emotion. "Of course I knew you wanted to work, don't you think I'm proud of you? Of what you've accomplished? At the same time, can I help it if I wish you didn't have to? I want to be able to support us, to provide for you in the way you're used to. I'd move heaven and earth for you, you know that. I can't be the kind of man you want, I guess."

The fire lighting his dark blue eyes dimmed, replaced with despair. "I don't have fine words and fancy manners you deserve. Hell, I never even understood why you married me in the first place, we're so different. I didn't want to think about it too much, but I guess I needed to. Maybe then I'd know what would make you stay."

"It's easy, Rafe." She dropped her voice to a whisper. "I know in your own way you love me, but...I need to be part of your life. Not a piece of fragile porcelain held at arms' distance, but nestled in a corner of your soul. And I need—" Looking over the extent of his property, she felt insignificant. This was what mattered to him, keeping the ranch, making it work. She was no more than a piece of the puzzle entitled *Rafe's Perfect Life*, like a tractor or brood hen.

Just as multiple generations of her family had practiced law and dallied in Boston's political arena, generations of Walkers had farmed and raised cattle on this land. Being a lawyer in Boston didn't make one a Fitzgerald, and marrying a Walker didn't make one a rancher. In truth, she felt no more an integral part of the holding now than she had when she arrived as a new bride, four years ago.

He'd needed her trust fund to help pull the ranch out of a hole the previous year, and her salary helped keep them in the black. Still, as he'd asserted in the heat of their most recent argument, the ranch wasn't in her blood.

To bring the point home—he'd never told her, but she knew it to be true—her name wasn't on the deed. She wasn't really a Walker. That was his implication, and his belief.

That was the way of life here. Men took care of the important things, such as supporting their wives and maintaining the family legacy. If they'd had children, maybe their relationship would have been different, but she'd wanted to wait. Then, she'd devoted so much effort to her job. The job he'd encouraged her to accept but now seemed to resent.

Shrugging, she said, "Maybe you're right. Maybe what we have isn't enough."

"It's all I have, damn it, all I can give. All I know how to give."

Cathy shook her head and walked to the driver's door of the Ford Thunderbird. If only he could say the right words, make the right gesture to change her mind. At this point she wasn't sure there was anything "right" enough.

"Wait!"

She stopped, hand on the latch, but she didn't turn. *Maybe, maybe...*

"Where will you be, you know, in case something comes up?"

In case something comes up. Not, "Where will you be in case I discover I can't live without you." In a nutshell, that was their problem and Rafe still didn't see it.

"If something should come up...?"

Her tone must have alerted him to her thinking because he lashed out. "You know what I meant."

"Yes, sadly, I do." She got in and started the engine, then lowered the window. "I'll be at The Hartman until I figure out what I'm going to do, and I'll be in the office as usual." Her work in the Hartman County prosecutor's office had kept her sane during the past year. It had also kept her away from home more than she'd expected. Her time at the office provided most of the grist for their arguments, but if she didn't feel comfortable at home, what else should she do but work?

One other time during the year, she'd packed her big Louie Vuitton Pullman bag. Before she even got it to the car he'd lured her back up to the bedroom where his probing, magic fingers and the incredible sensation of his thick cock slipping into her, blocked all other thought. Not this time.

The enormity of her actions weighed on her shoulders. She wanted to cry, to pound her hands on the steering wheel and scream in pain and frustration, but she wouldn't. Not in front of Rafe. Rafe, who loved her the only way he knew how but not the way she needed.

"It's someone in the office, isn't it?"

"What?" His question startled her.

"It's one of those lawyers you work with, a guy who knows how to dress and which wine to order. Someone from Boston or Chicago, who's anxious to take you back to the city." He spit out the words then waved his arm toward the road. "Well, go on, then. Go back to the high life in the East. I don't need you." Spinning on his heel, he stomped toward the barn, knocking his hat hard against his leg before slapping it on his head.

Her eyes burning with tears, Cathy raised the window and threw the car in gear. Gravel erupted from under the tires as the vehicle lunged forward, and dust filled the air. "I hope you choke on your words, Rafe Walker," she ground out, and thought she would choke herself from the ache constricting her throat.

The road into town ran straight, with nothing but the occasional lizard crossing from one side to the other to break the black ribbon. July heat rose in waves from the asphalt, obscuring the distant view as her tears obscured the near. They'd had no rain in weeks. The droplets running freely down her cheeks and off her chin were the most moisture their farm had seen since early May. Between her trial preparation and the drought, no wonder things between her and Rafe had come to a head. If only she could lay all the blame on weather and her first murder case.

With little to occupy her attention on the fifteen-mile drive, her mind drifted to when she and Rafe met and how different life had been.

€€€

"With any luck, Cathy, we'll catch ourselves a couple of cowboys tonight," Moira Kennedy said, as she smiled at a denim-clad man with smoky eyes and a black hat perched on his head.

He tipped the hat. "Ma'am."

Cathy grabbed her arm and dragged her forward, squeezing through the crowd at the bottom of the stands. "Moira, don't fall for the first cowboy you see. Besides, he's probably a law student like us, out playing."

The rodeo lights, noise and action had been exactly what Cathy wanted to celebrate her last night in Dallas before heading home to Boston. Not even the oppressive heat would ruin her fun. Her tight designer jeans bore no stains from hay or dirt or sweat, but they'd serve for one night of rodeo. Even less country, her ostrich-skin boots and white Stetson, under which she'd tucked her hair, screamed their newness, but she didn't care. Probably a good number of people milling around them had never been on a ranch. At least years in an equestrian club had taught her one end of a horse from the other.

"Face it," she told Moira, "we wouldn't know what to do with a real cowboy if one actually took the time to talk to us."

"Oh, I think I could figure out a few things." Moira looked over her shoulder, back toward the man tracking them with the sexy eyes.

After a rough summer and before a rougher last year of school, Cathy wanted to let loose. So, instead of attending the country club dinner dance to celebrate the end of her summer internship in Dallas, she'd passed up filet mignon and fine wine in crystal for barbeque on a bun and beer from a longneck bottle. For tonight, she'd rub elbows with ranchers, rodeo groupies and cowboy wannabees and forget about the importance of networking to a law career.

She had just crowded in at the fence demarcating the ring when the most handsome man she'd ever seen locked eyes with her from the back of a huge, black bull. The sounds and smells of the crowd faded to nothing.

Seven and a half heart-stopping seconds later, the bull tossed the cowboy to the ground like an irritating flea. Less than ninety seconds after brushing off his jeans, she looked up to find him by her side.

He stole her breath, her voice, her very thoughts.

Blue eyes so dark they seemed black shone from beneath thick, charcoal-colored lashes. He tipped back his dusty hat to reveal short dark hair. Dimples bracketed an impish grin. His body was lean and tall, and made even faded blue jeans and a worn denim shirt look good.

"Rafe Walker," he said by way of introduction, "and you are the most beautiful woman I've ever seen." If anything, his dimples deepened with the amusement in his voice. "I think I'm in love, little lady."

"Moira Kennedy." Moira hadn't lost her power of speech. She reached around Cathy to extend her hand. "That was very impressive, Rafe."

Something inside Cathy stirred at the way Moira said his name. *Raaaafe.* As though she whispered it after a long, slow session of fucking and the greatest orgasm in the history of the world.

"Nothing to it," he said. "Lots of guys better'n me."

"Oh, I doubt that," Moira murmured, moving beside him.

Rafe smiled at her, and then turned his gaze back to Cathy. "And your name is...?"

Somehow, in a practiced move but with calm she didn't feel, she arched her brows, flashed him a cool smile and held out her hand. "Catherine Fitzgerald."

He wiped his hands on his jeans, adding as much dust as he removed, and took her fingers in his. Warmth flooded her and her knees threatened to buckle. He used her hand to pull her closer, emphasizing how they fit together.

"Can I buy you a Coke?" Quickly he glanced at Moira. "Both of you, of course."

Cathy also turned to look at her friend.

Moira correctly read the almost imperceptible shake of Cathy's head. "No, I have someone to meet."

"You do? Who?" The two of them had come to the rodeo alone.

Moira smiled and flipped her dark hair over her shoulder. "Don't know yet." She tugged on Cathy's arm and turned her far enough away from Rafe to whisper, "Remember who said we wouldn't know what to do with a cowboy? Well, here." She reached into her shoulder bag and withdrew two condoms which she tucked into Cathy's hand. "This is in case the cowboy teaches you what to do."

"Are you nuts? I'm not going to get wild and crazy with a complete stranger."

"You never know. Make sure you call me if you're not coming back to the room tonight, and don't forget our flight is at eleven."

"Moira—"

But Moira fled. Back to Smokey Eyes, no doubt.

Giddy and breathless, Cathy faced Rafe Walker. Without another word, he led her toward the concession stand. When they had Cokes in hand, he guided her to an area at the end of the stables, behind the loudspeakers, where they could hear each other talk.

"So, this your first rodeo?" he asked.

"How did you know?"

He pointed to her legs. "Those aren't Levis. And those expensive boots don't look like they've been near a cow patty."

"Busted," she said with a nervous laugh.

He lifted her hat, releasing waves of hair to tumble over her shoulders and down her back. Rafe caught his breath and stared at it.

"To make your hat look lived in," he said in a hushed voice, "you need to beat it against your leg a few times. But holy God, why you'd want to cover up that hair with any hat is beyond me."

"Thank you."

"I'm going to kiss you, Miss Catherine Fitzgerald. Is that all right?"

He stepped closer before she had a chance to say yes. She set her cup on a stack of boxes. He tossed his into a nearby

118

trash can, never having taken a sip. Her hands walked up the front of his shirt and over his shoulders to meet at his nape. His hands fit neatly at the small of her back. He pulled her to him.

He was tall, but on tiptoe her body meshed with his in all the right places. Firm, warm lips met hers. When his tongue demanded she open to him, she did. His flavor burst in her mouth, spearmint and heat, as he boldly explored.

Raising his head, he looked around with heavy-lidded eyes. He walked across the yard, dragging her beside him. After a quick glance, he threw open a stall door and slipped inside. Moments after closing the gate, he lifted her, fitting her over his erection, scraping her breasts against his chest. She dug tunnels through his hair with her fingers, knocking his hat on the straw where he'd dropped her Stetson. Hungrily, she pulled his lips back to hers.

She whimpered. He moaned, licking the inside of her mouth as though she were the sweetest treat he'd ever had. The grind of his hips suggested what he wanted and she wrapped her legs around his waist. He took two steps to back her up to the inside wall. She twisted, rubbing her crotch into the bulge that seemed ready to burst through zipper and button and double stitching the jeans ads bragged about.

Rafe tore his mouth away even while they dry humped against the stables. She buried her face in his neck, oblivious to anything around them, ignoring all but the rising tide of incredible sensations spiraling outward from low in her belly. Her hips had a life of their own, slamming into his, grinding, rubbing, stroking, denim to denim, heat to heat.

His breath bellowed against her ear, sending tendrils of hair flying. "God, I want you."

He smelled of dirt and animal and raw masculinity. His neck was gritty with dust. She didn't care. Her tongue streaked a path up the cords of straining muscle to his earlobe. She nipped it.

"Yes." One word escaped, all she could manage as he shifted slightly and hit the right spot to send her over the edge. She gasped and held her breath, her head thrown back. Pinpricks of light flew across the blackness inside her lids.

Her nipples, sensitive and erect, pushed against the confines of her chambray shirt. The softness she'd admired when she bought the shirt that morning now seemed rough as sandpaper on her breasts. She should have worn a bra, but her small breasts rarely needed the support. Now the additional sensitivity helped prolong what had been an intense orgasm all on its own.

Finally, she came back to herself. Rafe's labored breathing matched hers, though the bulge in his jeans hadn't diminished. He let her slide down his body and then rested his forehead on her head. The sounds of people walking by penetrated her hearing and bright flames of mortification heated her cheeks.

"You're hot, Catherine Fitzgerald. I think I was in high school the last time I did what we just did. And unlike you, Becky Thomson didn't get off on it back then, though I shot off like a firecracker." He grinned down at her. "Guess turn about is fair play, though I sure would like to feel a little relief too."

She'd never done anything like that before, *never*. Not with her high school boyfriend to whom she'd lost her virginity, and not with the society lawyer to whom she was practically engaged back home. She'd had orgasms before, sure, but not with the primal passion she'd just experienced with this man she'd known about fifteen minutes. A piercing blaze had ripped through their clothing, without any touching or foreplay.

"I hardly know what to say, Mr. Walker. This should be so embarrassing."

He stroked her hair, twirling a strand between calloused fingers and staring at it in awe. "Call me Rafe. I think it's accepted etiquette for two people who humped like rabbits to use each other's first names."

"Humped...?"

"Umm-hmmm." He held her hair to his nose and breathed in. "Like rabbits. Though I think usually Mr. Rabbit isn't still hard and aching when they finish. Jesus, you smell good. Really good."

"You smell like bull, Rafe."

He burst out laughing and stared down at her, his dimples like shining beacons, calling to her. "You are all dusty and mussed. And so pretty I can hardly stand it. Come back to the hotel with me?"

"I don't even know you."

"I think we knew each other the minute you smiled at me across the ring just before the gate opened."

"I did not smile at you." She fingered his collar, thinking how much she'd like to be touching him instead of his shirt.

"Oh yes you did. I never flirt with strange women." She cast him a doubtful look so he added, "Not when I'm about to bull ride. But you...you were different. I knew right away we'd get together." He leaned down to her ear. "And I've never done this before. My partner's pleasure has never been so important. Come back to the room with me. Let's do it again only right this time. Let me make you feel good, Catherine Fitzgerald." In her ear, the words came out on a growl.

"Make up your mind, lady. I need this stall," came a voice from outside.

"Oh, Lord." She felt her cheeks blush crimson but Rafe just laughed.

Gallantly, he opened the stall door and ushered her out. Tipping his hat to the older man holding the rope on a very large bull, he said, "Thanks for the use of the stall, Ace."

"Don't make a habit of it," the older man groused.

"I promise," Rafe replied, smiling down at Cathy.

She wanted him again, right then and there. But naked this time. She wanted to be under him, feeling his weight, watching his muscles play in the light. She wanted to see his eyes when he filled her, as he rocked in and out and when he came, while deep inside her body.

"Is it possible we could do a little something in your car? Before getting to the hotel?"

He laughed. "Darlin', I'm happy to oblige. It's a truck and there is a *lot* we can do."

Fire pooled in her groin. Burning passion proved to be a familiar feeling that lasted through the weekend, barricaded in his hotel room. She called Moira after hastily rescheduling her flight. They didn't come up for air until Sunday night when she had to return to her room and pack.

Then reality intruded. Cathy returned to Boston and the conservative, ordered career path she'd laid out. She never forgot Rafe, though. Not his smile or his laugh or the way his light touch made her feel. Oh, yes, his touch.

All autumn she remembered the sensation of his calloused fingers brushing her skin. And the sweet sensation of his thick cock, wet with her own moisture, slipping into her, stretching, abrading, filling her. Each time they came together she wondered how it was that a man she barely knew made her feel complete, so unlike the other men she'd been with. She'd half decided by the time the weekend ended that she was in love.

Despite promises, he didn't contact her. All efforts to reach him ended in unanswered messages. She put a stop to the speculation that she would marry her high-powered boyfriend, but gave up all hope of ever hearing from Rafe.

In December and January, three phone calls from him punctured the cold, bringing the memory of a blazing Texas summer while snow fell outside her Boston window.

A month before graduation, she arrived from a late class to find him sitting on her porch steps, turning the wide brim of his Stetson in his big hands as he watched traffic pass. Their eyes met and he stood. When he spread his arms, she flowed into them like water filling an empty canyon after spring rains.

"I can't stop thinking about you," he murmured into her hair.

"Nor I, you," she responded, thinking how perfect life was at that moment.

He piled her books on the porch and then kissed her so she felt it in every inch of her body, unmindful of horns and shouts of encouragement from passing vehicles or giggles from pedestrians.

"Do you have your own room in this place?" Rafe had his arm firmly planted around her shoulders, but he looked up at the Victorian house behind her.

"I have the whole house." She smiled at the look of astonishment on his face. "It belongs to my grandmother, but she's out of the country right now."

He showed his dimples. "Well, God bless Grandma." Scooping her books off the porch, he followed her inside. Setting the books down again, this time on a table in the entry hall, he wasted no time taking Cathy in his arms.

She folded her arms against her chest and then pushed him away. "Wait a minute. You went months without contacting me or returning my calls. I know I just fell into your arms out there on the sidewalk, but why should I now?" Her heart lodged in her throat watching him tuck his hands in his back pockets, hang his head and stare at his boots.

"I was scared, Cathy." When he looked up she couldn't mistake the sincerity in his eyes. "That weekend in Dallas hit me like a two-by-four. I've never been so into a woman. No pun intended." He grinned for a brief moment. "We're so different; I didn't think there was a chance in hell we could make it together. But damn if I could get you out of my mind."

He reached for her hand and she let him take it. "Then when I called and we talked, and I still couldn't get past the lump in my throat with every thought of you, I gave in. I knew I had to see you, knew I had to find out if you feel anything like I do."

"And that is...?"

"You're on my mind all the time. I go out on the ranch and think of you, of that weekend. I go to bed dog tired, and can't sleep for thinking about you, wondering where you are, who you're with." He slapped his hat against his thigh. "Weren't you engaged or about to be engaged?"

"I broke up with him."

His eyes lit up. "You did?"

"As soon as I got back from Dallas. Somehow I thought a cowboy I met out there was interested in me."

"You were right, although he was too much of a jackass to follow you back here and beg you to come home with him. But I'm here now. Come to Texas when you graduate. Marry me."

"What?" She blinked, uncertain she'd heard right. "I can't marry you. I'm a city girl."

"The ranch isn't that far from Houston. When you feel the need for city, we'll go in."

"I don't know anything about ranching."

124

"That's my job."

"Are you close enough to a town that needs lawyers?"

"Fifteen miles away is the county seat. Where there's a courthouse there're lawyers." His smile broke out, dimples and all. "None as pretty as you, darlin'."

"I can't cook."

That stopped him. He studied her eyes. And her heart?

"You can read a cookbook, though?" At her nod he let out a breath. "Then we can manage. Hell, I've been managing alone for years. You'll have time to learn."

She heaved a sigh. "God, Rafe. I can't believe I'm even considering this." She looked away, nibbling her bottom lip.

Months ago, they'd lit up the world with their fiery passion. But they hadn't spent the whole weekend screwing around in bed. They'd talked for hours, sharing their views of life, both ridiculous and sublime. She'd thought maybe she found The One, until she returned to Boston and hadn't heard a word from him.

Her heart screamed to jump at the chance for happiness with a man who made her forget the world with his touch. Her mind pounded home the message that she didn't know this man at all. *One weekend of passion does not a happy marriage make.*

But it didn't guarantee a failure, either. Plenty of good marriages had been built on less. None that she could think of at the moment, but...

"Yes," she whispered.

He swooped her into his arms and twirled her. "Oh God, Cathy. I'll make you happy, I swear I will."

"I love you, Rafe."

He set her on her feet and held her close. "Cathy, Cathy," he murmured into her hair. "I love you too." Then he chuckled. "Just think. I'll be makin' love to the sexiest, most beautiful attorney in the whole state of Texas. And, darlin', you know how big Texas is."

He followed her up the stairs to her room. Sunlight spattered across the bed, filtered through the leaves of the beech tree outside the window. A hint of vanilla lingered in the air, a reminder of the candle she'd burned that morning while dressing.

Rafe's hands landed on her shoulders, halting them in front of her floor mirror. From behind, he reached around and unfastened the first button of her blouse. Gently, he spread the fabric. Almost religiously, his fingers skimmed the bare skin revealed.

He stepped closer. She leaned back, loving the sense of being enfolded, loving his scent—a primal, sexy, musk—loving the hard length of him pressed into her back. His chest rose and fell with each breath, the muscles tense, strong, warm.

With each button unfastened, he allowed his fingers to touch her skin, to explore, to revere. Finally he swept the material off her shoulders and to the floor. From the back, he unhooked her bra, but instead of stripping it off, he slid his hands around to cup her breasts.

"They're small," she said.

"They're perfect." As if to prove his words, he kneaded them tenderly and then played the nipples with his palms until they stood in super-sensitized points.

She rolled her head back and moaned. He bent his head and nipped her neck, never moving his gaze from their joint reflection.

It took only a few minutes for him to bare her. His hands roamed at will over her skin. Imposing his booted foot between her feet, he nudged her legs apart. With one hand, he reached for the golden triangle between her thighs, with the other, he caressed her breast.

"Rafe!" She wanted more, much more.

"Shh. Just watch."

And she did.

With infinite care he furrowed her pubic hair, teasing the length, twirling his fingers through it before continuing on his quest. His middle finger parted her labia, releasing a powerful waft of scent. He inhaled deeply.

Her arousal seemed to initiate a change. He rocked his hips; she pushed back, rubbing her bottom against his cock.

"No, it's too soon. I want to make you come first. Then I want to see you come again while I'm deep inside."

Her breath caught. His finger slipped in the moisture between her legs. He stroked up to her clit, bringing her fragrant wetness with him. Need built in her belly. She spread her legs farther apart and rolled her labia over his fingers, which were now moving back and dipping inside her slick passage.

"So wet. So hot. Mine."

"All yours," she said. The sparkle in his eyes when his gaze captured hers in the mirror stoked her fire higher. "Faster, Rafe. I want you inside me."

He pulled her nipple, then flicked it. She bit back a scream with the pain/pleasure. His fingers thrust in and out of her pussy, then pulled her moisture, dragged her pleasure, up to her clit, teasing mercilessly. Her hips jerked forward and back, riding his hand in front, rubbing his cock in back.

Like an itch she couldn't scratch, she worked her hips and arched her back to find relief. Every nerve ending sparked. Her breath came in pants. Her fingers stretched out as tension spiraled through her.

And then... And then, the dam burst. Relentlessly, his strokes hurled her into a flood of sensation. Her pussy convulsed around and over his fingers. Tremors rippled through her and she keened her release into the silence of the room.

"Look," he commanded.

She opened her eyes to see a woman in the throes of orgasm. A rosy hue covered her chest and neck. Her eyes glazed below heavy lids. Her nipples stood at stiff peaks, dark red and alert. And Rafe's fingers, wet and calloused, moved triumphantly, pushing, pressing, rubbing.

"God, you're beautiful."

She stretched her arms over her head and around his neck, pulling his mouth to hers. "*You're* beautiful," she whispered before meeting his lips and thrusting her tongue into his mouth.

Hungrily she ate at him. He turned her and at last let her unbutton his shirt and unzip his jeans, allowing his cock the freedom it craved.

She dropped to her knees and pulled his pants and briefs to mid-thigh. She crawled forward. Grasping him, she looked up while teasing the purple head with her tongue. Suddenly as greedy for his cock as she had been for his mouth, she took all of him in one movement.

He gasped and then groaned. His fingers tangled in her hair, stopping her from sliding forward. Holding his crown in her mouth, she looked up.

"Are you sure you want to do this?"

She took him in hand, sliding her fist to the base of his shaft, twisting lightly and then stroking back up.

"Absolutely. Let me suck your dick, Rafe."

He strangled out a laugh. "God, I love it when you talk dirty. You look so sweet and conservative and then you come out with something like 'dick'."

She smiled, feeling powerful. "Let me suck your dick and then you can drill my cunt. We can fuck all afternoon." He groaned and she chuckled. "Later we can do a sixty-nine and you can eat me. I'll swallow, Rafe, I'll take all of you down my throat and swallow what you give me. I'll let you—"

"Enough!" He grabbed her arms and lifted her up and over to the bed.

At once she scooted back and spread her legs. "Fuck me with your boots on, Cowboy."

"Yes, ma'am." On hands and knees he crawled between her legs. "Cathy, have you been with anyone since...?"

"No, have you?" She watched his eyes but they gazed at her clear and honest.

He shook his head. "It would have been a letdown, darlin'. Birth control?"

"Taken care of. Come and get me or do I need to think of more dirty things to say?"

"I hope you won't be thinking at all." He settled over her. Guiding his shaft, he ran it up and down between her lower lips, coating them both with her moisture. Then he did what she'd been dreaming about for months, he slid inside, filling her completely, stretching the lining of her pussy until she thought she couldn't take any more.

And he moved, slipping out, leaving only the head of his shaft inside and then slowly pushing, expanding her body and awareness. His mouth found hers and his tongue struck a rhythm to match his cock.

She spread her knees wider than she thought they could go. Her legs wrapped around his narrow waist. Arching her back scraped her nipples through the curly hair on his chest. She smoothed her hands up the backs of his arms to the firm muscles of his shoulders, which were tense and strained with the pressure of holding him over her body. Then she stroked down, along his spine.

A sheen of sweat coated his back. She felt a light moisture between them, too, and heard the slap of their bodies as they came together. Faster now, and harder, he glided into her. He had control of her body, of her senses. They breathed in synch. Their hearts beat together, dancing the ballet their bodies composed.

Her hands reached his buttocks. Grabbing his cheeks, she dug in her nails, kneading and pulling him even closer. She wanted to be one with him, she wanted him to know and feel what he did to her, with every nerve he had.

She got her wish when sensation cascaded over her at the same moment Rafe threw back his head and cried out her name. For the first time in her life, a man's seed spurted against the lining of her vagina. In seconds, sperm swam farther into her body, becoming part of her. Sexy, so sexy, to think they were joined in this way. The thought set off another orgasmic wave.

Long minutes later, Rafe lay beside her. She thought again about what they'd done. The man she loved had given her a portion of himself. This was a commitment, a way of showing how much they meant to each other. Someday they'd make a baby and then truly they would be one, in a new and unique way.

He propped up on his elbow and took her hand. Linking their fingers, he kissed her knuckles. "I can't wait 'til we're married. I want to be everything to you."

"You already are."

She looked into the eyes of the man who loved her, and saw the promise of their future. He was her destiny. If he lived in Texas, then Texas was her home too. If he lived on a farm, she'd learn to garden. And she'd learn to cook—such was her determination to be the best wife to Rafe.

ဆဝၵၵ

She couldn't have known then that no marriage maintained the level of wild desire they'd experienced in those heady, early days. It never occurred to her that she and Rafe would become little more than roommates who shared a bed. That they would brush by each other but never really touch, or that for weeks on end they'd be too tired for simple sex, much less romps of passion.

She longed for life the way it used to be, before her job took so much time and Rafe shut her out. She longed for what she hadn't had in a long time, and for something she feared she'd never receive from Rafe again.

Chapter Two

"Rafe?" To the uninitiated, his sister's voice sounded casual but her steely undertone tipped him off to trouble.

"Hey, Sis. How're you doing?" He put down the glass holding three fingers of deep, amber whiskey, his second in the fifteen minutes since the mailman brought the certified letter.

"I'm fine. The question is, how're *you* doin'? And Cathy. How's she?"

So this was the call, finally. Cathy had been gone almost two weeks. He was surprised they'd let him off the hook this long. He hadn't told anyone she was gone, figuring first it was no one else's business, and hoping second that she'd come home before her leaving became common knowledge. The former didn't seem to matter to his sister, obviously, and the latter simply hadn't happened.

Every day marked another high point in how miserable he was, but he hadn't contacted Cathy. He'd meant it when he said he wanted her to be happy, and if that brought him misery then so be it. Of course, before, he hadn't known the meaning of the word *misery*. He'd lived alone for years before they married, but the past two weeks had been different. Before, being alone had been his choice, a quiet house had meant peace after a long day's work. When Cathy agreed to become his wife, he thought he'd never be alone again, not in his heart, not in spirit.

Not like this.

The aching loneliness of the empty house, the burgeoning hope when the phone rang, the quick futile glances to the dirt drive to see if her Thunderbird was barreling home—all these things had sent pain lancing through him, but he'd borne it. The letter he'd received a little while ago stating Cathy was seeking a divorce was almost too much for him, though. He didn't know how he'd go on when everything good in his life had turned to shit.

There was no use hiding the facts any longer. A page and a half of typed truth stared at him from the table, right next to the open bottle and half-full glass. "Barb, Cathy's left me."

"I know, Rafe." Her voice was low, her words sympathetic, but the tone was still pure iron.

He huffed a breath. "I reckon the whole county knows by now." More than the whole county if his sister had heard. She lived in Houston, miles away. "She served me with papers today. She intends to divorce me."

A sharp intake of breath indicated his sister's shock. "Divorce? But-but that's crazy. I thought she'd just moved into town to think things through. That woman loves you. Anyone can 3cc it."

"Not Cathy, and she's the only one who counts."

"What do you plan to do about it?"

He pictured his mom standing right behind his sister, listening to every word and trying to get Barbara to give him advice. Their mother lived in a suite of rooms his brother-in-law built for her off their Houston home. Barbara would be standing in her kitchen, her back rigid and her blue eyes flaming, looking just like their mom.

"What do you mean what do I plan to do? The thing I want most in the world is for Cathy to be happy. Evidently, I don't make her happy. What do you think, I should drag her back here and have her hate me for it? I can't do that. This time, she made it clear she—"

"What do you mean 'this time'? She's left before?"

Hell! Why hadn't he just told the whole Houston contingent that he'd take care of his own business?

"We've had a few problems over the last couple of years, but we've always been able to deal with things. With no outside help," he emphasized. His hint fell on deaf ears.

"Is it work? Sex?"

"Barbara, if you think I'm discussing my sex life with you, it's time we checked into nursing care because you're senile." He added a light tone but his sister didn't laugh. Hoping it didn't reflect the despair infecting his spirit, he lowered his voice. "Really, there's nothing you can do. I appreciate the concern, but I think this time we're finished. Cathy misses the city. You know, she's educated and sophisticated, and I'm...well, I'm not." He didn't explain his worst fear, that Cathy might want another man.

In almost a whisper, Barbara repeated his latest statement. His mother's voice rose in the background and Barb added her own comments. "Nonsense. You're educated. Maybe you didn't go to Harvard, but the University of Texas is a fine school. I know Cathy comes from a different background, but I never thought she minded the simpler lifestyle. She loves her job, and I know she loves you. Let us think for a minute."

"There's no reason for either of you to think. I can—"

"Is there someone else?"

His heart sank. "Not for me." Rafe stared with longing at the whiskey waiting on the table. He rarely pulled the bottle of Jim Beam out from the back of the cabinet, but he was looking forward to getting good and drunk tonight. He wished he could start right away, but one slurred or false word and Barbara would blab to their mom that he was drinking. God knows, those two might jump in the car and drive up, and that was all he needed.

Silence. "Do you know for sure there is for her?"

"Not for sure, no. But she's been working long hours with one particular guy and there're lots of private phone calls when she's home. She says I need to figure out what I want, and she says it like she already knows what she wants. The fact that she left shows it's not me."

"So, what is it, did she say?" His mother said something too low for him to hear. "Just a minute, Mama, I'm waiting for him to say," Barb whispered in an aside.

Subtle, Barb. "No. Maybe I needed to say I love her more, or maybe she wants me to sweep her off her feet. Hell, after four years I can't be expected to kiss her hand every morning or get down on one knee to ask what's for dinner. Half the time lately she's not even home for dinner until eight o'clock, but I don't complain. I understand she's building her career." Anger replaced despair as he remembered that he thought Cathy was having an affair which would account for her late nights.

How could she do that to him? To them?

He remembered clear as day when she'd hired on as the first female DA in Hartman County. Skidding that Thunderbird to a stop at the edge of the pasture, she'd blown the horn and waved. Then she'd run out to where he was mowing. Having exchanged heels for tennis shoes, she'd still worn one of her expensive Boston suits that she'd put on for the interview. He'd found out she left stockings and panties at home when she climbed on the tractor and straddled him.

Lord knows where they found room between the gear shift and mower controls, but somehow she unzipped his jeans and climbed on. She didn't care about the suit skirt pushed up around her waist or that he'd tossed her jacket onto the cut grass so he could suck her tits. She didn't even care about the traffic passing on the highway a few hundred feet away. She'd only cared about celebrating with him, in their own special way.

Even now he could feel what it was like having her slide down his dick. The sun beat on the roof of the tractor and there was no breeze, making the day feel well over the one hundred and two degrees the weatherman had predicted. Sweat ran like a river and slicked their bodies. Cathy tasted salty and hot. She'd said she liked him dirty and sweaty when they made love, and she'd nipped his earlobe. He drove deep into her liquid heat, coming like a volcano. She screamed his name out in that open field with the smell of sex and cut grass enveloping them. And he'd loved every minute of it. Why hadn't they ever done that again?

"Rafe? Rafe Walker!"

Oh shit. He'd fantasized about having sex while his sister was on the phone.

"Sorry. I got distracted."

"I asked if anything else had happened. We just don't see Cathy having an affair."

Damn. "I didn't want to worry you but we almost went bankrupt last year."

"Oh no!"

He heard "bankrupt" and "wait a minute" as Barb relayed the information.

"Between this damn drought and the drop in cattle prices, we came close to not making it. I had to ask Cathy for money from her trust fund to pull us through. It almost destroyed me," he admitted, ashamed. "A man shouldn't have to go to his wife for help like that. And then, I've been putting in lots of hours,

136

trying to keep our heads above water. Truthfully, we don't see each other much anymore. Maybe this is best."

"Rafe, Cathy's money is your money. I'm sure she feels that way. Just like the ranch is hers as well as yours."

Of course, the ranch wasn't Cathy's. He'd never put her name on the deed. Somewhere in the back of his mind he'd never really believed she'd stay. He'd never thought what he offered would be enough, and he was right.

"She's not like you and Mom."

"Of course she isn't. You don't want her to be. You want her to be like Cathy, like herself. Why don't you two take some time away? Beau and I sure need a break from the house and kids, and so did Daddy and Mama. Why do you think we spent weekends at Gran's every few months?"

Definitely more information than he wanted.

"I have to face it, Barb. I'm a failure as a husband."

Her silence cut him like a knife. She must agree.

"Is Cathy right, Rafe? Do you *really* not know what you want?"

In her quiet question he found the answer.

৯৯৯

Two weeks gone—well, twelve days and fourteen hours—and Cathy had heard nothing from Rafe. Each morning she rose from her bed hoping he'd call that day to talk about getting back together. Each night she turned out the light with a heart aching from loneliness.

During the day she performed at her peak on her first murder case. In the evenings, she concentrated on the next day in court to avoid thinking about Rafe and what a failure she was as a wife. And she must be an awful wife because she couldn't find a way to make Rafe love her again.

But nights were the hardest. Then she tossed and turned, remembering what life had been like when they shared impromptu passion. The stress of too many long hours preparing for court over the last few months had come to an end with the guilty verdict that morning. Now she'd have too much time to stem the tide of the good memories.

Like when he'd surprised her one Saturday afternoon. He'd come into her home office freshly washed from the barn. He'd stripped off her slacks and knelt on the floor, her legs over his shoulders. He'd teased the insides of her thighs with the bristles of a five o'clock shadow and then used his tongue to lap her cream and tantalize her clit until she exploded against his mouth.

Just as good were the summer evenings when they sat on the porch drinking iced tea and watching the sunset. Words weren't necessary to her peace, just Rafe's closeness, in spirit as well as body.

All of that had changed when the ranch came close to failing last year and he'd come—practically hat in hand—to ask if she could help. They were married, so of course she wanted to share her money. But some small part of her had resented his asking because he'd never made her feel they were partners when it came to the Walker property. She had lawyer's work and he had rancher's work, which, as he'd phrased it, was their livelihood. As though her job was a hobby. Maybe she should have taken the hint then, and left.

And now she had. The divorce papers had been served yesterday. Even that hadn't prompted Rafe to call. With the case over, she'd start applying for positions back in Boston.

To celebrate their win, her co-counsel, Mark Connors, had offered to buy lunch at The Hartman Inn. Cathy knew he was attracted to her. He'd made several veiled comments about how he'd like to know her better. Mark, with his knowing good looks and rampant ambition, was the kind of man she'd almost married, the sort who'd lost all attraction for her once she'd visited the dusty, dry plains of Texas. Everything changed with Rafe, and now no smile or quip from Mark sent even a small tingle down her back.

At the end of the meal, Cathy excused herself. Mark was headed back to the office and she had calls to make from her room.

"I enjoyed working with you, Mark."

"I liked working with you too. I think we make a great team."

Oh, Lord, he didn't really wink, did he? "Well, maybe we'll be on a case together again sometime." She held out her hand, not expecting him to grasp the chance to pull her into an embrace. She pushed away, but not before she felt him stiffen. She followed his gaze and saw Rafe.

Her heart raced and her breath caught in her throat. Ignoring Mark, she turned and focused on the incredible man a few dozen feet away. She wanted him with a fierceness even stronger than when she'd seen him waiting on her front step in Boston years ago. And she hadn't thought any wanting could be greater than that.

He stood transfixed in the entryway, watching them. With his rigid posture, Cathy knew every muscle hidden beneath his best suit had tensed. The gleam off his boots shone in the artificial illumination of the chandelier but there was no welcoming sparkle in his eyes.

Except for the restaurant lighting, the room was dim, and a glance out the window showed the previously sunny sky filled with dark clouds. Rain, she thought. Then she took another look at Rafe's face. *No, a storm.*

He stood so still he didn't even seem to breathe. Cellophane-wrapped roses hung from his hand, at least a dozen and blood red. Dressed as he was, she imagined he'd gone full-bore for romance, sophisticated Boston style. Cathy thought daisies, brown-eyed Susans and even Texas bluebonnets were as romantic as roses, but she wouldn't argue the point, if he ever got through the doorway and to the table.

Cathy sensed Mark step away from her, a move that Rafe could easily interpret as guilt. She started forward since he didn't seem inclined to take the first step.

A clap of thunder broke the tension. With a jerk, Rafe looked out the window then back at her. Pain, and then rage, filled his eyes. His stance and expression rivaled the tormented sky, and she knew right then he wouldn't ask her to come back to him. Seeing her with Mark would have verified his worst fears about her and their marriage. He confirmed her thought when he thrust the roses at the hostess, spun on his polished heel and strode out.

At least rain would make his life easier. She wouldn't have to worry about him or the ranch when she left.

"Rafe!" She ran after him, desperate to explain. He might leave, but she didn't want him to think she'd been unfaithful.

Cathy reached the door in time to watch her life speed away in a black pickup truck.

Chapter Three

Rafe slapped the steering wheel with the heel of his hand as he sped through a yellow light at the edge of town. He was right, Cathy was seeing another man. And she didn't even have the decency to take it out of town, to hide the affair from prying, gossiping biddies in the place where he lived and had to do business. Damn her! Damn her to Hell, along with that wussy-looking bastard she was fooling around with.

After talking to his sister, he'd called his lawyer and requested he add Cathy's name to all his property. Early today he'd signed the papers, now burning a hole in his inside jacket pocket. Then he'd gone in search of the biggest bunch of roses he could find. At last, he'd walked to the courthouse in search of Cathy. He'd arrived to find her case ended, so he'd gone to her office. That's when he heard she was having lunch at the Inn.

And the Inn was where he'd discovered her in another man's arms. He was right after all. She was having an affair.

At seventy-five miles an hour, his truck ate up the distance to the ranch. He almost dared a trooper to stop him today. He'd end up in jail for assault because he was going to hit the first person who got close to him. Glancing up at the darkening sky, he mused that the only good thing happening today was the rain.

Finally. Rain for the fields, to fill the streams and cisterns. From the appearance of the sky, maybe this storm would provide enough water for weeks. He desperately hoped so. He not only needed the water for the ranch to recover, but he was determined to pay Cathy back every cent she'd taken from her trust fund. No way would he be beholden to her, now that she wouldn't be his wife any longer.

Although Rafe's mind overflowed with images of that blond jerk's arms around Cathy, other thoughts pushed their way to the forefront. There was much to do before the full force of the storm struck. He had to make certain the horses had entry to the barn and that they had clean hay, that the equipment was under cover and the house was battened down. The rain was welcome, but a bad storm could bring a lot of damage too. Strong wind already pushed his truck around the road.

He tuned the radio to the local agricultural station. "...is a warning. Tornados have been spotted in Harrell and Hartman counties. One is confirmed to have stayed on the ground for at least twenty-five miles. These funnels are large and dangerous. If you are in Hartman, Williams, Sayors and the surrounding areas, take cover immediately. This is a warn—"

Punching the button to silence the announcement, Rafe slammed his foot on the brake, bringing the truck to a fishtailing stop. His heart pounded. White-knuckled, his hands grasped the top of the steering wheel where he dropped his head. Seven miles ahead of him lay his life, land and buildings that had been in his family for generations.

No. Not true. The truth had hit him like a punch to the gut yesterday. Ahead of him lay his business. His life was eight miles behind him in the form of a blond, green-eyed woman whom he loved with everything in him. And who might have no idea of the upcoming danger.

142

Without another thought, Rafe U-turned and raced toward Hartman. He didn't slow when rain pelted the windshield, but he had no choice with the onslaught of hail.

At last he pulled up in front of the hotel, flung open the truck door and dashed into the lobby. Hotel guests stood at the windows watching the storm. Rafe strode to the front desk. "There're tornado warnings out for the area. Everyone should head for shelter."

"Tornado!" The girl behind the counter stared at him with wide, frightened eyes. An older man appeared from a back room and Rafe explained again in terse sentences. He asked the girl, "Do you know where Mrs. Walker is?"

"N-no. Maybe the restaurant?" Her voice cracked with ready tears.

He'd been gone less than half an hour. Could she still be in the restaurant? He ran in that direction.

The room was almost empty and Cathy was nowhere in sight. He hurried back to the desk, now crowded with staff listening to instructions from the manager. "What's Mrs. Walker's room?" The girl stared for a moment. Rafe slapped the counter. "Mrs. Walker's room!"

"Oh!" She clicked some keys on the computer. "Two-twenty."

Rafe dashed for the stairs. At the second floor he first turned the wrong direction, then reversed to find the correct door.

"Cathy!" He pounded but didn't hear a sound coming from inside. Where would she have gone? Back to the office? To the guy's place?

No. He pushed the image of her in another man's arms to the back of his mind. Right now what she had or hadn't done didn't matter in relation to her life.

He rushed back to the lobby where—thank God—he saw her standing with a group of people at one of the windows.

He hadn't noticed earlier, but she wore his favorite emerald green suit. The shade brought out the spectacular color of her eyes and turned her hair the color of wheat. Today she had the golden strands pulled back into a low bun. On Cathy the style looked sexy rather than matronly. She'd never needed heels for height—she was a mere four inches shorter than his six-foot-two frame—but she wore them because he'd told her once that he couldn't take his eyes off her legs when she had them on. Rafe didn't want to contemplate who'd been staring at her legs today.

"Cathy!" He launched himself toward her.

"Rafe! What are you—?"

"There's no time to explain." He grabbed her hand and started for the door. "Come on, we have to get out of here."

"Where are we going? It's raining—"

He stopped her words with his lips. Not a kiss like he wanted to give her, but one to send a message, a promise. That's what he hoped, anyway. "God willing, we're going home. Okay?"

She gave a nod in reply. It was enough.

Despite the high heels, she kept up with him as he darted out the front door. In seconds, he headed the truck out of town and went speeding toward home again.

ഇൽഇൽ

Cathy had never been so terrified. Hail covered the road, turning the asphalt into a slippery, treacherous mess. Rafe guided the truck with skill she'd never before appreciated. Rain

144

started again, falling in torrents that the windshield wipers couldn't begin to handle. Belted in, she still felt sick with fear. She couldn't see where they were driving, and didn't think Rafe could either.

She chanced a glance at him. They hadn't said a word since he'd told her at the hotel he was taking her home. She wished she knew what changed his mind, though it hardly mattered at the moment. The feeling of relief that flooded her with his statement surprised her, although she'd been dying to hear him say something like it for the last two weeks. She wanted to explain that she knew what she wanted. Not telling him before had been not only wrong, but holding in her feelings had cost them a year of possible happiness.

He couldn't spare a second for her right now, though. Totally focused on the road and the truck, he leaned forward as though being closer to the windshield would allow him better visibility. His hands gripped the wheel and his mouth formed a tight, thin line.

Suddenly, the rain lessened, and with that, so did the tightness in her chest. "Better," she said.

It felt like hours since they'd left the hotel. She turned to look out the back and was surprised to see the lights of Hartman not far behind them. They hadn't driven nearly as far as she'd thought. The high roofline of The Hartman Inn was visible, but a low cloud covered it as she watched.

"Shit!" The expletive from Rafe startled her.

"What is it? You can see better now, can't you?" She fought to keep anxiety from her tone, but Rafe's expression made it difficult.

He turned his head for a brief look at her. Her fear must have shown clearly on her face, because he reached over to squeeze her hand and flash her a quick smile. "It seems we're among tornados, darlin'. When I came into town today I'd hoped to stir up a storm of emotion in you, but I didn't have this in mind."

"Tornados?" Frowning, she looked off to the right, where the ranch was located. She sucked in a breath. Far off in the distance, a narrow, dark gray funnel stretched from the cloud cover to the ground, skimming the earth. As Cathy watched, the tip of the funnel rose then touched down again in a different spot. "My God, Rafe, it could hit the ranch."

"That's not what I'm worried about right now." He leveled his gaze at the rearview mirror.

Cathy swiveled to look out the back window. The thick cloud she thought contained only rain was actually... "Oh my God!"

"I've got to get you to safety," he muttered.

That couldn't be a tornado. Everyone knew tornadoes were funnels, large at the top, tapering to a point at the bottom, like the one she'd seen heading toward the ranch. But the swirling air mass behind them suddenly tossed debris into the air. Sparks arced, like fireworks in the dark sky.

"Transformers," Rafe said, pressing the accelerator to the floor even while watching in the mirrors as the town behind them destructed.

"This can't be," Cathy breathed. "There won't be anything left."

"Worried about your boyfriend?"

She snapped her head around in time to see him wince. So he did believe there was something between her and Mark. "There is no boyfriend, only a colleague."

He looked chagrined. "It doesn't matter. I shouldn't have said anything. No time to worry about that now." He clamped his lips together, the same lips that had sent desire coursing through her fifteen or twenty minutes ago.

Unable to stop herself, she turned back toward Hartman, but the town had disappeared. A swirling mass of charcoal-colored air followed them with remarkable speed.

Rafe twisted the wheel to the right, slipping and skidding in the mud of a dirt driveway. They'd caught up to more rain and he seemed to throw the truck into 4-wheel drive and flip the windshield wipers on high simultaneously. The vehicle groaned, then found traction. They flew up the drive, running perpendicular to the onrushing tornado.

"Where are we going?" Cathy shouted. A small tree branch blew across the hood. She clenched her hands and tried to keep from panicking.

He kept glancing past her to measure their distance from the storm. Cathy peered through the rain and saw a house ahead.

Rafe whipped the truck around the building. "Come on!" He turned off the engine and opened the door. Jumping to the ground, he looked to see if she followed. She did, though her heels sunk into the muddy surface, slowing her progress. The wind disposed of her chignon, and fierce rain battered her before she reached the back steps.

Rafe pounded on the door then turned the knob, but the house was locked. He breathed heavily and scrubbed his hand across his cheek. "Wait here," he yelled over the screaming wind.

She tucked herself as close to the door as possible and watched as he tested the windows along the back. A gust tore the lid off an aluminum trashcan and hurled it, catching Rafe's shoulder and head. Cathy's hand flew to her mouth but too late to stop her scream. Rafe stumbled and then straightened, looking dazed. He shook his head and sent her a weak smile, which did little to stop the terror throwing her heart into a dizzying rhythm.

Please, God, please don't let anything happen to Rafe. I love him.

She opened her eyes to see him rip off his jacket and wrap it around his forearm and hand. He swung his arm in a wide arc and broke a window, then swept the frame clear of glass. Hiking himself up, he took a breath and lifted his leg over the sill.

Within seconds he was at the back door, dragging Cathy into the house. Debris sailed by, driven by the wind. Papers, leaves and twigs detoured into the house through the broken window and open doorway.

Rafe grasped Cathy's elbow with one hand and opened every door he found with the other, quickly discovering there was no basement.

Suddenly, a roar captured her attention. There had been no tracks outside, but a train was blasting its way toward them. Several somethings—she had no idea what—banged into the side of the house. Glass shattered, wind whipped around them. She couldn't hear herself think. She certainly couldn't make herself heard by Rafe, couldn't tell him how much she loved him, how she regretted they'd ended this way.

Rafe dragged her in the direction they'd come, back into the bedroom. Grabbing the bedspread, he swung open the closet door and thrust Cathy onto the floor. He wrapped the spread around him, pulled the door shut, and then dropped over her, covering them both with the heavy material.

She thought her ears would burst before it all ended. The closet door popped open; the very walls shook. Rafe cried out in pain, frightening her more than all the noise and wind. Her only comfort was his weight pressing her to the floor, and the knowledge he was with her. Even if they died there on that closet floor, she owed him her life in more ways than one. If only she could tell him.

Everything went still. Immediately. One moment she imagined she lay between the tracks of the California Zephyr, pummeled with noise and anything the wind threw at them. The next moment...nothing. No wind, no sound. In its way, the silence deafened more than the noise.

In the stillness, she sensed Rafe—his scent, his breath on her hair, his arms wrapped so tightly around her she could hardly breathe. *Thank you, God, thank you!*

He stirred, pushing back on his haunches. He turned her over and looked down. "Are you all right?"

"I think so. Are you?"

"Yeah." His gaze raked her, full of concern. Lightly, his hands roamed down her arms, bringing her palms up to his lips.

"Rafe, look." They lay in the closet space, but she saw him clearly. When he pulled her to her feet she registered the emptiness around them. The entire back wall of the house had disappeared along with most of the side and front. The destruction was too much to comprehend, and she sank to the floor again. Rafe crouched beside her.

"You're bleeding!" He ran his fingers back down her arm exploring for the damage.

She frowned, examining him first with her eyes and then, gently, with her hands. "No, it's your blood. We've got to get you to a hospital."

The arms of his shirt hung, shredded and crimson-stained. His head bled freely where the trashcan lid had hit him. Gashes criss-crossed his back from where objects had cut through the bedspread, driven by the ferocity of the wind.

"I'm okay, as long as you're okay." He held her hand to his lips. When he looked up, his eyes had filled with tears.

"You saved *my* life." She could only whisper.

"I saved my life. Without you, what would I have? What would I be? That's what I came to tell you."

"Your ranch! Oh, Rafe, you could have made it home if you hadn't come back for me. What if—?"

He kissed her. "Hush, darlin'. If *our* ranch is still there, we'll consider ourselves blessed. If it's not..." The pain in his eyes tore at her heart. "Then we'll still be blessed, for this second chance."

She cradled his cheek and nodded. "I love you. Only you, always you."

He closed his eyes and leaned his head against hers. "That's how I feel, how I felt the moment I looked up from that bull and saw you. If I ever go a day again without telling you, it's not because I don't feel it." He stood, pulling her up with him. "I'm sure the truck is gone. Do you want to wait here while I try to find help?"

"No, where you go, I go. I don't want to let you out of my sight again, ever."

He looked down. "You might change your mind after a few feet in those shoes."

"That's true. Maybe—" She tilted her head at a sound coming up the drive.

Rafe made his way toward what would have been the front of the structure, stepping around broken boards and overturned furniture. A beat-up pickup made its way toward them, swerving around debris.

"It's Sam Matthews, coming to see if anyone's here, I guess." He heaved a sigh and raked his hair, then winced.

"Do you think he'll take us to the hospital?" Rafe was right. Trying to go anywhere in her heels invited disaster, but she didn't want him to leave her alone.

"I don't want to go to the hospital."

"No?"

He shook his head and gave her a quick, heated kiss. "I do know what I want, Cathy. I want to be everything to you. I want to prove you're everything to me. I just hope we have a house left to start over in."

He jumped the few feet to the ground and went to meet Sam, never seeing the glisten of joyful tears in her eyes.

Chapter Four

Rafe climbed from the rickety truck. "Thanks, Sam."

Cathy leaned forward in the center of the bench seat, trying to see through Sam's mud-spattered windshield.

"Ain't no problem." Sam Matthews peered through the windshield too. "Don't look too bad, Rafe. Mebbee you got lucky."

Lucky? He looked at his beautiful wife, knowing she worried about their house and how he would take it if they found the worst had happened. "I'm the luckiest man alive, Sam." Cathy swung her head around to stare at him. She smiled when she saw he was watching her, not inspecting the property.

"Yeah, you gist might be," Sam said, still looking around for any damage. "Well—" he jammed the old truck into gear, "—I reckon I'd better see if I kin find if anyone else needs help. Tornaders missed our place all together, so if you need anything, give a holler."

Rafe leaned in and scooped Cathy up in his arms. "We'll do that."

Cathy twisted around to look back in the truck. "Sam, if it looks like we made it through, I'll call you. We have room if someone needs a place to stay."

"That'd be great, Cathy."

She slammed the door shut and Sam pulled away while Rafe carried her to the porch. He set her on her feet and together they looked out. Tree limbs littered the yard. The azaleas bordering the house were in shambles and none of Cathy's carefully planted flowerbeds remained unscathed. A lawn chair blown in from somewhere lay battered against the porch.

"This is nothing," Rafe said. "Maybe we were missed by the bad stuff." He could hardly believe the brunt of the storm passed them by.

"I hope so."

"If you'll check the inside, I'll walk around the outside and then see about the barn." He squeezed her hand and stepped off the porch.

An inspection of the house exterior showed no damage and his spirits rose with each minute. The barn fared well too. A tarp blown away by the wind left a hundred bales of hay exposed and scattered, but the structure suffered no damage. Neither had the animals inside. Before he could examine much more, Cathy joined him. She'd changed into jeans and a tee-shirt.

"The house is fine," she said. "I can't believe we weren't hit. After what happened to that other house, I... Rafe, we'd have had nothing."

He held her. "Everything that's important is standing right here. We could rebuild the house, the barn, anything else. Can we rebuild our marriage?"

"We made it through a tornado. Anything else should be a snap." She rose on her toes and kissed him. Her tongue traced the seam of his lips and he opened to her.

With her hands around his waist, she tugged him until she'd backed against the horse stall. She broke off and smiled. "The first time we made love was in a horse stall, remember?"

He smiled too. "What I remember is that it wasn't what I call making love. There were too many clothes between us."

"You fixed that soon enough."

"*I* did? You were the one who asked if we couldn't do something in the truck." He stroked her hair. Even after the rain and dirt and mud, her hair still smelled like flowers. When she'd left him, he buried his face in her pillow night after night just to capture that fragrance.

"I couldn't get enough of you. Then or now." She smoothed her hands over his arms, frowning again. "I'd suggest we do something right here except we should clean and bandage those cuts."

"What cuts? I don't feel any cuts." He leaned in for another kiss. Cathy had brushed her teeth or used mouthwash or something. Her mouth tasted minty and fresh. And hot. His tongue played with hers, his lips moving ever so lightly. Just enough to show her his hunger.

He cupped her butt, scraping his hands on the rough boards of the stall. She wrapped her arms around him timidly, and he wanted more. "Don't hold back, darlin', please. I almost lost you. I need you now."

As though his permission was all she needed, Cathy unbuttoned his shirt in record time and pushed it off. Little wounds on his back and bigger ones on his arms tore where blood had dried, but he didn't feel a thing except fire building inside.

"The heat seems worse than ever now that the rain's past," she said.

"I'm feeling a little hot, too," he murmured, dropping kisses on her hair as she tried to unbuckle his belt and unzip his slacks.

"You *are* hot, Cowboy."

He stepped back to push his pants below his thighs. Cathy had pulled off her tee-shirt and was working on her jeans. She wore no bra. Her nipples had already hardened. A tendril of hair stuck to her neck where she'd started to perspire. Rafe pushed her hair back and licked her neck. Salty, sweet, all Cathy. A taste he'd never tire of.

ೞೞೞ

If Rafe kept kissing her she'd never get out of those damn jeans. She laughed with the thrill of it.

"Hey, you're all cocked and primed, and I can't get undressed like this."

Grinning like a fox in the henhouse, he bent down and stripped her jeans and panties to her ankles. She toed off her tennis shoes and pulled her feet through the pants legs. In seconds, Rafe lifted her against the slats of the stall. She wrapped her legs around his waist.

His cock nudged her, seeking her sheath. The scent of her arousal hung heavy in the air and she knew she was wet. Then unerringly, he slid home.

Rafe groaned in her ear. "I love you."

"God, I love you too."

He squeezed her butt cheeks, kneading her skin, moving in and out. Her nipples grazed his chest with each thrust until she wanted to scream from pure pleasure. Without finesse, he pounded her into the boards, scratching her back on the wood.

She wanted it, wanted a little pain to match the pure pleasure. The tension that presaged an orgasm had started the minute Rafe said he needed her. She was close to coming already and he hadn't been in her for more than a few seconds.

Rafe's lips roamed her neck, shoulder, collarbone and back to her neck. His tongue licked and stroked, leaving fire wherever it touched. She panted. Her hands roved through his hair, glided across his shoulders, wet from sweat. His strength had saved her that afternoon. He'd covered her with his body and held her with a grip that was strong and sure and full of his love.

He thrust hard and she came, wildly, completely, letting go of the fear she'd felt earlier, relinquishing the pain and loneliness of the past two weeks. She convulsed around him, pulling him into her, milking his cock, welcoming his release and taking it as her own.

This was her man and her life and she wouldn't let him go again.

Later, when they'd dressed but still smelled of sex because there was no breeze to carry the scent away, he led her back to the house. His arm stretched across her shoulders and hers wrapped around his waist. They strolled, in no hurry, though the rest of the ranch waited to be inspected for wind and hail damage.

"The papers for the ranch were in my jacket. They're probably plastered against some house in Timbuktu by now."

She stopped to smell one yellow rose left unbowed on her favorite bush. "Why did you have ranch papers?"

"For you to sign. I had your name put on everything. I should have done it sooner, right after we got married. I'm sorry I didn't." He looked away from her, as though embarrassed.

Talking was impossible with her heart lodged in her throat. "Rafe, I…"

He smiled at her. "We can talk about it later."

She nodded, fighting tears.

"I guess I'd better change clothes and go out to check the herd and pastures."

"Without the truck, what will you drive out there?"

Dimples in full force, he grinned. "The tractor made it through the storm."

Thank God, so had they. Both storms.

"I have fond memories of that tractor. Maybe I can come with you?"

He laughed. "Why, darlin', I'd love that." They walked up the steps and into the house. *Their* house.

We're so much luckier than most, she thought. Not because they could afford to repair whatever damage they might find, though they were fortunate in that regard.

No, they were lucky *because* of the storm. They'd found a new burst of energy for their marriage and life. Runners call it second wind. Without the tornado, Rafe might not have come back for her. If he hadn't, Cathy wasn't sure they would have made it.

As it happened, they'd reforged a vow. One spoken at their wedding, but which now held meaning they couldn't have understood then. To love each other. Forever and ever, whatever wind might blow.

About the Author

Prior to writing her first fiction only a few years ago, Dee S. Knight lived a varied lifestyle. Her high school sweetheart promised excitement when they married. When they tied the knot after college, he delivered. She's been a house parent for wards of the court, an assistant librarian, gift wrapper, long distance trucker, high school teacher, adult ed teacher, technical writer, clerk, computer consultant and...romance writer, which she's enjoyed the most. For the past many years, Dee and her honey, a software consultant, have lived all over the United States, enjoying each new place while looking forward to future locales and discoveries. Currently, they reside in the Great Midwest.

To learn more about Dee, please visit www.deesknight.com.

Hunk of Burnin' Love

Veronica Wilde

Chapter One

Vanessa Reeves woke up naked and alone on a muggy summer morning with her thoughts full of Elvis Presley. It was August sixteenth, the anniversary of Elvis's death, and that reminded her of her boyfriend, Landon. Or rather, her ex-boyfriend. Landon had ended their three-year relationship at the beginning of summer, saying he wanted to be free. She still couldn't help thinking about him, though, especially on hot lonely nights when it was just her in bed, naked and burning for his touch. Or on lazy mornings like this when she dreamt of sleepily rolling over to guide him inside her. They had been so good at morning sex. And sex in the shower. Sex outside in the garden—that too. And sex in her backseat that one time—

Stop, she scolded herself. She would never get over Landon if she kept thinking about their sex life. Yet it was hard not to. Landon had been the ultimate bad boy, six feet of bad attitude and good looks, with serpentine tattoos and the irresistible smile of the devil himself. And the sex—oh, the things he could do with those long fingers and gyrating hips. Memories of him burned through her like molten lava.

Quickly Vanessa forced her mind back to neutral territory—Elvis. Despite the fact that he had died years before she was born, she had always loved his music. Landon had made fun of her Elvis collection, calling her *Grandma* and pretending to check her dentures. *You're twenty-six,* he'd say. *Why do you listen to that oldies crap?* She liked other music. She just liked Elvis a lot too. She never understood why Landon had to be so sarcastic about it, as if the earsplitting industrial bands he worshipped were somehow musically superior.

Now she couldn't listen to Elvis without thinking of Landon.

Vanessa stretched out between her white sheets. Her window was open and she could tell by the breeze that it was a muggy, overcast morning—perfect for staying in bed with a hard, well-muscled body that knew just how she liked to be touched and licked...

Stop it, Vanessa.

Reluctantly, she climbed out of bed and looked in the mirror. Almost unconsciously she cupped her full, firm breasts then ran her hands down the narrow curve of her waist. She'd been working out all summer, determined to make Landon burn with regret over leaving her. Now she was strong, buff and curvy in all the right places. Her long black hair had never looked so glossy and her deep tan made her brown eyes glow. Unfortunately she hadn't run into Landon once all summer— and to make matters worse, she hadn't had a date since they broke up. Plenty of guys had asked her out at the bookstore where she worked but none of them felt right. Her best friend was starting to refer to it as her "Summer of Celibacy".

She would die before she let Landon know it but she had spent most nights this summer listening to Elvis's love songs, wishing fervently to meet someone new. Somehow Elvis had a song for every emotion. "All Shook Up" described perfectly Landon's physical effect on her. "Kentucky Rain" captured her anguish after he left. And of course "Heartbreak Hotel" and "Are

You Lonesome Tonight" epitomized every solitary night this summer.

Now she was facing another weekend without a man, but she didn't want to think about that. Instead her mind turned to her mom, who had also been a major Elvis fan. In honor of the date, Vanessa decided to visit her. She slipped on jeans and a white tank top, then headed off to the florist.

ಸಂ∞ಸಂ

Hours later she was walking through the cemetery with pink tea roses in her hand—her mom's favorite. It was a gentle summer twilight, birds singing in the huge maple and elm trees that adorned the grounds. A few other families were visiting but the cemetery was quiet. She glanced to the west, where the setting sun was casting long shadows through the spiked iron gate.

She walked past the meditation pond and mausoleum until she came to her mother's grave. *Carole Reeves, beloved wife and mother.* Vanessa blinked back her tears. Her vibrant, fun-loving mother had died of breast cancer four years ago and she had never stopped feeling the basic unfairness of it all.

"Hey there, darlin'."

She turned to see a middle-aged man behind her. Instinctively she clutched her handbag and glanced around to make sure other visitors were still present in the cemetery. Then she took a look at his jeans, sweatshirt and baseball cap and relaxed. This guy just didn't seem menacing.

In fact, despite his sunglasses, he seemed downright familiar. Probably he was the cemetery caretaker, here to remind her that the gates would be closing soon.

"Oh—hello. Is it closing time?" She glanced again at the sunset. "I didn't realize the time."

"No, no, you're fine. I'm just saying hi."

His deep southern accent was also familiar. So was his voice. He almost sounded—ridiculous as this was—like Elvis Presley. She had Elvis on the brain today.

He nodded at her mother's grave. "That your momma?"

"Yes. She passed away a few years ago. Breast cancer." Tears rose to her eyes and she tried to brush them away.

"I'm sorry to hear that. Losing your momma is a terrible thing. I lost mine young too."

Just like Elvis, she thought. The more this guy talked, the more he sounded exactly like him. On the other hand, the silver hair poking out from his baseball cap, and the portly belly pushing at his sweatshirt, didn't exactly evoke the popular image of the sexy, raven-haired star.

"I'm sorry," she told him. "Was it cancer?"

"Heart attack."

A peaceful silence settled between them as they regarded her mother's grave. A faint breeze stirred the grass as the man adjusted his baseball cap. She glanced sideways at him. Yes, his resemblance to Elvis was remarkable. He could have been a middle-aged, pudgy Elvis gone gray. Just like Elvis would look if he were alive.

Be real, she scolded herself. Elvis had died decades ago and he had been in his early forties then. He would be an old man now—if the legends about him hoaxing his death were true.

But this man was in his late fifties at the most. Maybe a well-preserved sixty. Still she glanced curiously at him. Finally she had to say it.

"I'm sure you hear this all the time," she began, "but you look just like Elvis Presley."

The man didn't smile or even look at her.

She waited for a response. The man lifted his head and stared right at her. There was just enough light in the cemetery for her to see through the dark lenses of his sunglasses...and right into his pale blue bedroom eyes, just like Elvis's. She looked at his lips. Elvis had always had the most distinctive lips, sensuous and unique, even after his weight gain.

So did this man. A shudder ran through her.

"You a fan?" he said at last.

She nodded fervently. "My boyfriend—ex-boyfriend—always made fun of me for listening to him but I love him. I like newer music, don't get me wrong, but Elvis's music just—it was perfect."

Those blue eyes bore through the sunglasses. "Sounds like you take him serious."

"Of course I do," she said, surprised. "He's the King." Her eyes ran nervously over his pudgy chin and cheeks, his silver hair. Silly, silly to be thinking these things.

"You ever seen one of them impersonators?"

She made a face of distaste. "No. I think it's sort of disrespectful..." Then she realized the obvious. "Oh my God. You're an Elvis impersonator." Certainly he wasn't dressed as such right now but he had to be. He just looked too much like him not to be. Perhaps he'd even had plastic surgery to get those perfect lips.

The man broke out in a broad smile. "You hear of the Celebrity Star Revue?"

"That show with all the celebrity impersonators? The one at the summer carnival?" She had seen the ads on TV but never thought of attending.

"Come on by the show tonight. In fact, come on backstage and see me, I'll get you a great seat."

"For real? I would love that."

The man still had an odd light in his blue eyes. But all he said was, "See you tonight then. Nine o'clock."

Chapter Two

Every summer the carnival came to town, perching on the edge of the beach like a loud, multicolored monster of whirling rides and cheap prizes. Vanessa hadn't been there in years, namely because Landon had always made fun of it. *Childish* and *stupid,* he called it. Yet now it seemed like fun—cheap, bawdy fun. As she walked through the straw-covered grounds, the electronic song of the merry-go-round and the screams of joy from the rollercoaster overwhelmed her. She could smell fried dough and cotton candy and everywhere she looked someone was trying to shoot moving bottles or stumbling off the Tilt-A-Whirl.

Yes, it all sparkled before her like a vulgar, roaring gem. Suddenly she realized how much she had missed out on this summer by staying home and moping over Landon. Well, that was going to change—starting tonight. She was wearing a short red cotton dress that showed off her tan legs and her long black hair was loose; the appreciative glances of passing men told her she looked good. So what if she was alone? Feeling adventurous, she headed down to the auditorium where glossy posters advertised the Celebrity Star Revue.

She paid for her ticket and slipped down a dark hall leading backstage. "Hi, I'm Vanessa Reeves," she told the security guard. "Mr...." Her confidence died as she realized she had never learned the impersonator's real name. "Elvis invited me to come see him tonight. He told me to come backstage."

"Did he now." The man looked her up and down with a sly smile. "Go down that hall there. Second door on the right."

"Thank you so much." Even without directions, she would have known which dressing room was his. A booming rendition of "Burning Love" was blaring through the door. She knocked.

Was that a "come in" she heard? She tried the knob and stepped in—and found herself staring at a naked man.

Her first impression was of smooth, tanned muscle. He was in his mid-to-late twenties, just over six feet tall with the broad shoulders and narrow hips of a model. That flawless sun-browned skin just seemed to go on and on, rippling from perfectly carved pectoral muscles down to a sculpted abdomen and continuing into long, hard-muscled legs. But as if magnetized, Vanessa's eyes were drawn to the center of his body, where an impressively thick, long cock was growing hard under her gaze. A wave of shock and heat swept over her and she quickly dragged her attention up to the man's face.

Silky black hair framed one of the most handsome faces she'd ever seen. Ice-blue eyes blazed at her in outrage.

"Oh God, I'm sorry," she gasped. Heart pounding, she began to back out.

"Sorry?" the guy yelled, grabbing a towel to cover himself. "Haven't you ever heard of knocking?"

"I *did* knock," she said hotly. "I thought you said to come in. Look, I'm sorry. The guard said this was the Elvis impersonator's room."

It was obvious now that the portly, silver-haired impersonator she had met at the cemetery was nowhere around. Her face was burning pink with embarrassment—and her body was flushed with reactive lust at seeing such gorgeous, naked masculinity.

He snapped off the boom box, cutting off the Elvis song mid-tune. As he wrapped the towel around his narrow hips, his gaze traveled up and down her body. "Looking for Elvis, are you?"

"Yes." Despite her flustered state, she couldn't help noticing just how fine he looked in the towel. With his wide shoulders and sculpted torso, he could have stepped out of an underwear commercial. "Look, I'm really sorry. I was at the cemetery today and met him—"

"You met Elvis at the cemetery?" A mocking white smile crept across his tanned face. "Was he eating a peanut butter and banana sandwich? Did he say, *Thank you, thank you very much?*"

She scowled. "Look, I happen to be a big Elvis fan. So while I'm sorry I walked in on you—well, naked—I'm not going to let you mock his memory."

Somehow her indignation unlocked his true smile. He grinned more genuinely and came toward her. "That makes two of us. T.J. Woodard here—a huge fan of the King."

She mustered a friendly smile, as if he wasn't standing before her with just a white towel tenting over that impressive manhood. As if the image of his enticingly stiff cock wasn't flashing repeatedly in her mind no matter how hard she tried to think of something innocent. "Vanessa Reeves. Thanks for being so nice about the mix-up."

T.J. adjusted his towel as he walked closer. For a moment she stiffened with anticipation. But he only pushed the door shut behind her.

Her heart began to race with a nervousness that wasn't entirely unpleasant.

"So," she said lamely. "Do you work here as part of the crew?"

Those blue eyes were mesmerizing her with their erotic speculation. With every moment that passed, it was becoming harder to remember the Elvis impersonator she had come here to see.

"Yeah, I work the lights." His gaze was growing more interested, yet calculating too as he took in her short red dress, then returned to her face. "So how about I get you the best seat in the house?"

"Okay..." A devious hint rode his smile but she wasn't sure how to decipher it.

He leaned closer. "Just on one condition."

Something fluttered inside her stomach. She nodded in a daze.

"You have to give me the best kiss I've ever had in my life." His lips were full and sexy and she couldn't help but notice how pink they were against his tan. "Deal?"

She swallowed nervously. "Deal," she promised, her voice barely a whisper, and extended her hand.

T.J. took her hand in one meaningful squeeze. Then he let go of his towel.

Unable to stop herself, her gaze fell down his broad golden-brown chest to the eight-inch rod stiffening between his legs. It rose up like a velvet colossus, straining toward her with undisguised lust.

A helpless, animal heat swept through her like wildfire. All the frustration and yearning of this sexless summer collected between her legs in one trembling, demanding ache.

"I..." Her voice was shaking as she tried to assert control over the situation. She hadn't even had a date in months and now here she was under the spell of a naked stranger. Normally she would never do something like this, no matter how sexy the man. Yet she only leaned back against the door as T.J. took her skirt and pushed it up her thighs. Taking his cock in his hand, he rubbed its swollen head back and forth over her panties. Vanessa closed her eyes and succumbed to the moment, feeling the heat of his skin press through the satin.

"You still haven't kissed me yet," he whispered.

Her fingers shook as she took his perfect, taunting face in her hands and kissed him on his jaw. Her mouth traveled up his skin, her lips tracing the line of his high cheekbones before grazing his eyelids. He was so blood-stirringly gorgeous that her body needed to adjust to him before addressing the ultimate prize of his mouth. She lightly bit his nose, then kissed each of his silky temples. She could smell the scent of his shampoo and it mingled with something feverish—the hot smell of masculine arousal. At last her fingers slid down to his collarbone and she rested her forehead against his, not quite letting her mouth touch his.

He half-opened his burning crystalline eyes and stared at her in a challenge.

She brushed her mouth over his, learning the fullness and curve of his lips before testing their sensitivity with her tongue. She bit his lower lip just once, letting it escape her teeth so slowly that he moaned. Then her lips moved together in a simulation of a pucker as she kissed him traditionally for the first time.

He pushed her hard against the door, kissing her back as passionately and feverishly as a man gone mad. His rigid cock pressed into her panties as she twisted and ground against him. Hungrily his hands slid into her long black hair, pinning her head to the door as his mouth worked hers in ravenous need.

A pounding on the door separated them. "T.J., soundcheck."

Vanessa jumped away, wiping her mouth. A flush of arousal stained her cheeks and dampened her panties. She wasn't sure what had just happened but she knew it wasn't anything she'd experienced before.

T.J.'s eyes burned into her. "They need me. Come find me after the show, okay?"

Wild horses couldn't have prevented her. She nodded, and with another tricky smile, he slipped into his pants and headed out.

Catching her breath, Vanessa tugged down her skirt and walked back down the hall. The guard wordlessly led her into the auditorium to a table up front as the rest of the audience filtered in.

Five minutes later, the ceiling lights dimmed and a voice boomed over the speakers, "Ladies and gentlemen, welcome to Celebrity Star Revue."

A thrill-building hum raced through the room. From the same speakers a lively music began as four girls in skimpy costumes took the stage in a wild dance. The announcer boomed, "And here's the King of Rock and Roll...Elvis Presley!"

The band launched into a merry rendition of "Viva Las Vegas". Vanessa turned expectantly toward the stage to see at last her older cemetery friend.

Yet the Elvis who strolled out in a black and gold lamé jacket and massive sunglasses was young. His black hair was cut full with sideburns and he strutted and moved with snake-hipped finesse. He was the young sexy Elvis, the one whose gyrating pelvis had been banned on *The Ed Sullivan Show*. The one whose lazy bedroom eyes and erotic pout had caused millions of young girls and grown women to scream and faint with excitement over his overwhelming sexual charisma.

It was T.J.

Vanessa's jaw dropped as she watched her backstage man move as smoothly as the suave Elvis she had seen in all of her mother's favorite old movies. His voice, deep and confident, was almost an exact replica of Elvis's voice. How was that possible? He had sounded nothing like him in the dressing room—not that she had been using her ears as much as her eyes, of course. He had Elvis's height, and black hair and blue eyes, but his features were very different. Yet somehow his transformation into Elvis was complete.

"Viva Las Vegas" ended and he disappeared offstage. An older emcee emerged and, taking the microphone, introduced all of the band members and revue dancers. The band launched into the rollicking opening chords of "Burning Love".

T.J. sauntered back out in a black leather jumpsuit. He was no longer wearing sunglasses and she could see those crystalline eyes perfectly as he sang. For the first time, she understood the meaning of the word *heartthrob* as their gazes connected and her heart gave a desperate pang. *Stop it*, she scolded herself. *You don't even know this guy.* Yet she couldn't deny that he was affecting her emotions now as turbulently as his touch had affected her body just minutes earlier.

Still singing, he walked down the stage steps and into the audience. She watched in disbelief as he slid down to one knee in front of her and twisted his scarf round her neck as he sang.

After the refrain, T.J. pulled her toward him with the scarf and kissed her. There in front of the hundreds of envious, interested eyes watching him, his full mouth pressed hers in a momentary reawakening of their backstage fire—and then he was gone, still singing, back up to the stage.

She sat absolutely still in her seat, feeling as if her body had been turned to water or stone. For the rest of his performance, as he performed "Suspicious Minds" and "Heartbreak Hotel", she could not move. Her panties clung to her wet, aroused sex and her mouth burned where he had kissed her. And all the while her mind raced in a dazed question of what would happen after the show. Was T.J. simply playing a game with a fan who had stumbled into his dressing room or did he feel the same intensity between them that she did?

At last he left the stage and a Madonna impersonator came on. Vanessa barely took notice of her or the other performers until the show finale, when all of the impersonators took the stage for a final bow. T.J. emerged last and waved to the crowd before exiting, receiving the loudest applause. As the lights came up, Vanessa followed the rest of the crowd out to find the impersonators lined up behind a velvet rope, posing for photos.

Almost a dozen girls were giggling around T.J. He winked at her, then pulled a sneer for the camera. At last the crowd dispersed and she approached him.

"Hey, baby," he said in his best deep Elvis voice.

In his stage makeup, sideburns and black leather, T.J. loomed over her like a hybrid of the naked man she had kissed backstage and a suave young Elvis Presley. The effect was disconcerting. It made her want to follow him backstage to rewind the night—take off the jumpsuit and wipe off the eyeliner and sideburns until he was that same delectable naked man she had kissed.

She finally found her voice. "Why didn't you tell me backstage?"

"Now what fun would that be?" he asked in his normal voice. He was smiling casually but the heated challenge in his eyes still burned.

A group of middle-aged women appeared behind them with cameras. He flashed a perfect Elvis sneer at them, making one of the women shriek with excitement.

"I have another show," he told Vanessa without breaking character. He slipped her a piece of paper with an address on it. "Meet me at midnight for a swim."

It wasn't a question or a request but a command. As he posed for photos, Vanessa quickly walked away, the paper clenched in her shaking fingers.

Chapter Three

So. It was a hot August night and she had a date.

Not just any date. She was going to have a tryst with the sexiest man she'd ever met—a man who had pulled up her skirt and teased her with his hard cock moments after they met. A man who brought her every sexual nerve to life with one glance. He just happened to be an Elvis impersonator.

Her Summer of Celibacy was about to erupt in flames.

The August moon was high in the sky as she drove to his address. T.J. lived in the countryside and his road was lit only by the stars and the lights of distant houses. She shifted uneasily in the car, aware of her bikini bottoms already clinging to her wetness. She was wearing cut-offs and a pink tank top over a white macramé bikini that hugged her curves. She knew she looked sexy yet the memory of T.J.'s demanding mouth and prodding erection had her stomach fluttering with nerves.

She hadn't been with anyone since Landon broke up with her. Now she was facing a night with a man who affected her more strongly and swiftly than anyone she'd ever met. It could end in the summer romance of her dreams or it could end in her second heartache this year—but either way, she was determined to take the risk.

At last she pulled into his driveway and emerged to a chorus of crickets. A splash broke the peaceful summer night and she walked around to the back of the house.

Underwater lights illuminated a large backyard pool. T.J. was waiting in the greenish glow with a devilish grin, his black hair wet. The waves sent a dancing light over his tanned chest.

"About time," he said and splashed water at her.

"Hey!" She jumped back as the water sprinkled her tank top. "You're getting me wet."

"That is the point, I believe, in swimming."

"Not when I still have my shirt on."

"In my opinion, tank tops usually look best when wet." He splashed her again.

She dragged her attention from the impressive spectacle of his chest, determined to gain control of the situation. Slowly she pulled her pink tank top over her head and tossed it on the grass. She was gratified to see those blue eyes go hot with interest as the white bikini top rode up the bottom half of her breasts. She casually tugged it down with just enough force to almost reveal her nipples. She swallowed a smile as T.J. made a soft noise in his throat. Unzipping her cut-offs, she slid them down her hips with a suggestive swivel.

Her white bikini glowing against her tan, she descended onto the top underwater step.

"Stop right there," T.J. said. "You aren't coming in any further dressed like that."

She looked down incredulously at her bikini. "What?"

"You saw me naked. Fair's fair."

"You—" Words failed her as she realized the implication. "That was an accident," she protested. Did he honestly think she was going to just strip naked for his enjoyment before she'd even gotten in the water?

Apparently.

"Take off your top and your bottoms," he told her. "Now."

An inexplicable shyness swept over her. "I barely know you..."

He walked toward her. As he did, the pool grew more shallow and the water receded down to his hips, exposing his thickly erect cock. The underwater lights glistened on his naked body.

She bit her lip, unable to take her eyes from his straining erection.

"Come on, Vanessa," he cajoled in a voice that was half coaxing, half warning. He walked closer, the water dipping down to his thighs now to expose a set of tight, large balls. "Performing gets me so hot that I always need a swim afterward. And swimming feels best naked."

Her fingers shaking, she untied the strings of her bikini top. She held the fabric over her nipples for a moment, then gathered her courage and tossed it aside, her breasts bouncing with the movement. Her face was burning with self-consciousness as his hot gaze locked on her stiff rose-colored nipples. Forcing her thumbs into the waistband of her bikini bottoms, she eased them down her hips. Then she stopped, paralyzed by doubt. She couldn't help but be aware that this was the first time she had gotten naked with a new man in three years—and that she was doing it with a sexy performer who had his pick of women. She took a deep breath, wondering again if he felt as smitten as she did or if he simply did this all the time.

T.J. walked onto the bottom underwater step and stroked a casual finger through the curls exposed over the bikini bottom.

Without a word, he pressed his mouth to her stomach and delivered a kiss that burned the tanned curve of her navel. Slowly he began to lick down into the soft mound beneath her bottoms. She closed her eyes from the intensity of the sensations.

He bit each of her hipbones lightly before his tongue continued its southward path. Her tan lines glowed in the reflection of the pool, a white triangle of skin exposed against the dark olive tan of her stomach and thighs. For the first time she realized he had lowered her bikini bottoms without her feeling it. She twisted slightly, experiencing a shiver of longing as his tongue traced her bikini lines. Part of her was paralyzed with pleasure, breathless to see what he would do next, and a lustier, more impatient part of her wanted to throw a leg around his neck and pull his face straight into her pussy.

His tongue traveled between her legs for the first time, licking the moisture that had gathered from her excitement and the humid night without touching her most sensitive nerves. Unable to stop herself, she wiggled with yearning. But T.J.'s hands only slid up the back of her thighs, stroking her softest, most hidden skin until she felt as if her body were melting in his hands.

His fingers gently coaxed her thighs apart. His pale eyes were feverish with lust as he gazed up at her.

She looked down at him, breathing hard. Her bikini bottoms were twisted around her knees and he held her thighs apart in his hands. She was entirely in his control and could only pray that he would deliver the kind of earth-shaking satisfaction his eyes and lips had been promising all night.

He pressed his mouth to her pussy in a light, shivery kiss. The kiss turned long and hot as his lips moved over her folds with burning skill. She moaned, gripping the pool ladder to steady herself on the top step as an electric flush spread over her skin. Then, like an underwater serpent emerging from its cave, his tongue slipped between her lips, tasting her slick sweetness before pushing inside her to explore her most sensitive walls.

She moaned again, feeling her knees give way under the lust rocketing through her body. Weak with desire, she held onto the ladder for balance as T.J. pulled off her bikini bottoms and hooked her legs over his shoulder. Spreading her thighs wide, he moved his tongue over her with a skill and intensity she had never known. Her nipples were stiffer than they'd ever been in her life and they ached to be touched as his lips moved over her clit and sucked it gently.

"Yes, just like that..." she whispered. T.J touched her so confidently, as if he possessed the intimate knowledge of an old lover while thrilling her with the exquisite freshness of someone new. The sensations evoked by his mouth catered to her body's desires perfectly. This was fire. This was magic. No man had ever made her body come alive like this.

His tongue swam over her clit, making her blood rise, then swirled around her delicate hood in maddening circles. "Please, T.J., don't stop..."

She didn't resist as he pulled her down into the water. Almost all of her body was floating in the pool now, only her hips elevated in his hands as he licked and stroked her. She gripped the ladder handles and let her long hair spread out around her, succumbing to the power of his mouth. The cool water lapping against her bottom made the fiery tension of her pussy feel all the hotter, and the waves washing over her body teased her stiff nipples. Wordlessly begging for relief, Vanessa squirmed under his lips.

His tongue dove back inside her, illuminating all of her secret desires. She thrashed openly in his hands now, a white-hot tension filling her skin like a storm. T.J.'s tongue danced over her lips, sucking them together in a tender kiss, then ran up to titillate her clit. As he slid two of his fingers deep into her tight heat, he began to lick her with rough, rapid strokes in time with the staccato of his fingers.

A deep, urgent heat rolled through her body. As she looked down at his handsome face framed by her open thighs, her gaze connected with his in a moment of mutual lust. Her orgasm broke over her like lightning, convulsing her body and arching her back as her flesh throbbed beneath his mouth.

T.J. held tight to her twisting hips as she came. A hot flush was soaking her hair and face, her breasts stained pink from the heat of her orgasm. Slowly, shakily, she eased back from him and dipped her burning body in the cool water of the pool.

When she surfaced, T.J. drew her to him. "You okay?" he murmured, his mouth skating over hers.

"More than okay." She took a deep breath and tried to compose herself. It wasn't like her to connect so swiftly and deeply with anyone, let alone a man she had just met. The chemistry between her and T.J. was as unusual as it was thrilling. Even now, being held in his arms felt way too natural. She looked in his eyes, their brilliant color offset by his wet black lashes, and tried to gauge his feelings.

"What are you thinking?" She flushed with regret as soon as she said it. Men hated that question. Landon had always reacted with irritation when she asked him.

Yet T.J. only smiled and pulled her close, until her breasts flattened against his chest. "I'm thinking that my summer just got a lot better."

She rewarded him with a deep kiss, tasting herself on his mouth, and wound her arms around his neck. Satiated as she was in some ways, she still needed more of him—his body, his gaze, his mouth. She needed to feel all of him pressed up against her, his hard cock pushing between her thighs.

He kissed her back more sweetly than before. She closed her eyes and surrendered to it, thinking of all the different ways this guy knew how to kiss, from their dressing room kiss with his erection teasing her panties to his performance kiss during "Burning Love" to the way he was kissing her right now. His mouth knew tricks her ex-boyfriend had never heard of.

T.J. drew back from her and swam into the deeper end of the pool. She followed.

"So," he said. "You never said how you liked the show."

She didn't care if she sounded like a fawning groupie. "It was awesome. I never would have gone to something like that on my own but you blew me away."

His lips twisted in a wry smile.

She studied his face, the greenish pool lights dancing over it. His sensual lips belonged on an angel—but his brilliant eyes were full of the devil. He didn't look at all like Elvis right now and yet he emanated that same burning, lustful exuberance that he had given off so intensely during the show.

She cocked her head. "It's funny... Your features aren't much like Elvis, except for the coloring and your pouty lips, and you don't sound like him when you talk. And yet tonight you really delivered."

"I try. Anyone can put on black sideburns and big sunglasses and a jumpsuit, but that to me is just a parody. I try to bring forth the fire and charisma that made Elvis's performances so stunning."

"From what I saw tonight, you definitely do." She remembered then how they met. She had been so focused on T.J. that she had forgotten who invited her to the show. "So what's the deal with the other impersonator? Do you trade nights or something?"

T.J. shook his head. "No idea what you're talking about."

"The older Elvis," she prodded. "The one I met today at the cemetery. He's the one who told me to go to the show tonight."

T.J. gave her an odd look. "There is no other Elvis, Vanessa. It's just me."

"Seriously?" Now she was confused. "This guy was a dead ringer for Elvis. It was really something."

"Hold on. Are you telling me that some guy was dressed up in an Elvis costume at the cemetery? What were you doing there, anyway?"

"Visiting my mom's grave... She died a few years ago from breast cancer. And no, this guy was just wearing jeans and a baseball cap. It was his voice and his face. Just like Elvis would look if he'd gone gray."

"Elvis was already gray when he died. He colored his hair." T.J. swam close to her. "I'm sorry about your mom," he said and kissed her cheek.

"Thanks. She was a great lady." She appreciated the genuine sympathy in his eyes. Her ex-boyfriend had always been disinterested in the subject of her mom's death yet T.J. had shown greater compassion after only knowing her a few hours.

Still she couldn't stop thinking about the other Elvis. Perhaps it was another impersonator who admired T.J.'s performances. But those eyes—that voice... "Do you know other impersonators?"

T.J. was kissing her neck but now he pulled back. "Actually we prefer to be called 'tribute artists' and no, I don't. What's with this other guy? You're not one of those crazy Elvis fans who go to conventions and hang up pictures of him, are you?"

"Of course not. I just like his music. But this guy today—"

She saw the jealousy in T.J.'s eyes and stopped.

"Never mind," she said, kissing him again. "He led me to you and that's what's important."

"Is it now..." His tongue slid over hers. They kissed slowly and deeply as he framed her cheekbones in his hands. Then he tugged her back into the shallow end. As he pulled her against him, his mouth traveled to the hollow at the base of her throat. Her pulse beat against his lips.

T.J.'s hands wandered down to cup her breasts, stroking her nipples until she moaned. Hungry to feel him against her, Vanessa ran her hands over the cheeks of that tight, perfect butt she had admired on stage. T.J. responded by pushing her ample breasts together and sucking both of her nipples into his hot mouth.

A whimper of need escaped her. She threw her head back, surrendering to the spell of his lips on her breasts. The full summer moon filled her gaze, glowing and mystical as a chorus of crickets spread through the country night.

Something hard and hot and alive pressed insistently at her stomach. She looked down with a smile to find T.J.'s cock, swollen with demand against her.

He moved her long wet hair off her face. "See what you do to me," he whispered and wrapped her fingers around his shaft.

It throbbed in her hands like a hot, insistent animal. She stroked it with sensual fascination, loving this proof of his physical need for her. She palmed his head, wrenching a tight gasp of appreciation from him, as a wet flood of anticipation unleashed itself between her thighs.

T.J. began kissing her again, moving her back toward the pool steps. His hands roamed over her breasts before possessively cupping her pussy in his hand as she backed up the steps. Now they were in the same position they had begun this passionate night—her standing naked on the top step while he gazed up at her in lustful adoration. But this time he walked up the steps to stand equal with her.

Holding his shaft in his hand, he began to tease her clit with his swollen head just as he had in his dressing room. Immediately all the pent-up desire of their first encounter was renewed, flooding through her body like hot scarlet light. Vanessa leaned her head on his shoulder with a moan, letting tantalizing anticipation swell in her blood as she savored the firm feel of his cock. His muscles were so hard, yet trembling against her with what she sensed was the same desperate hunger.

Taking her hand, T.J. led her out of the pool. He retrieved a condom from the pocket of his discarded jeans then led her into the darkness of his backyard, away from the pool lights. She followed, hindered by the swollen wetness of her sex.

They kissed hungrily, feverishly, pulling at each other's bodies until they fell on the soft grass. Bathed in moonlight, Vanessa straddled him, feeling his cock push against her aching sex like a promise. This was the point of no return for her; she knew that in opening herself up to him, she was opening herself up to the full power of the connection she had sensed between them in the dressing room. She stared down into his shining eyes, then positioned him between her folds.

T.J. reached for her hips. Slowly she moved onto him until his head pushed past her initial tightness and deeper into her velvet heat. Smoothly she guided him in until their bodies were sealed together. She began moving on him with a corkscrew motion of her hips, teasing him until he groaned.

Oh God, she thought. *It's too good. He feels too perfect.* Her pussy was still wet and aroused from her earlier orgasm, lending an almost excruciating sensitivity to her flesh. As he drove into her with eager thrusts, her entire body felt incandescent.

Leaning forward, Vanessa began to fuck him with a smooth, expert rhythm, creating a luscious friction between them. T.J.'s cock seemed impossibly engorged inside her and an electric current was spreading through her blood, making her feel crazed with desire. Using her thigh muscles, she rode him as wild and fast as an untamed horse, meeting each thrust of his narrow hips with the answering tightness of her pussy. T.J. bucked wildly beneath her, his hands pawing at her ass in almost desperate need.

The ecstasy consuming her body was too intense to last. Vanessa fought for control. Without warning she released him from her snug heat, eliciting a howl of protest from T.J., and reversed her position. Holding onto his legs for support, she slid his cock inside her until he was engulfed once more as she faced the other way. She began to ride him again with that same smooth rhythm, reveling in the thrusts of his swollen head.

That sensual fire roared again through her body, blotting out all sensation except the hard, urgent drive of T.J.'s cock.

Groaning with excitement, he cupped her bouncing behind in his hands. Vanessa balanced herself on his shins, panting and delirious as she fucked him faster and harder. The friction of his cock driving in and out of her was making her dizzy with elation. T.J.'s balls were high and tight beneath her and a thunderous tension was swelling between her legs; she knew it wouldn't be long before either of them exploded.

Rising up on her knees, she began milking his cock with her inner muscles, making T.J.'s breath come fast. Her clit was a swollen nub between her legs and she ached to stroke herself, but instead she reached down and began to fondle T.J.'s balls. Lightly dragging her fingernails across his sac, she teased and rolled them in her hands as she slid up and down on his shaft. The combined sensations were too much for him. With a primal moan, he pulled her back on his chest and fingered her clit. Hot joy flooded Vanessa's body. Oh yes, this was the lover she'd been waiting for all her life. This was the man who knew how to touch her and take her and make her come. As he stroked her burning nub with a perfect rhythm, her pussy contracted in deep, wrenching spasms. Vanessa cried out in an almost painful ecstasy and felt her muscles close around his cock again as T.J. erupted deep inside her.

T.J. rolled onto his side, holding her in his arms. Their wet skin was covered with grass and sweat, their naked bodies blue in the moonlight. Vanessa felt suffused with erotic bliss. No one had ever lifted her to such heights. Yet she was afraid to speak and break the spell between them.

At last he pulled her tight to him and kissed her hair. "I've never met anyone who made me feel like this," he whispered.

She rolled over to look into those starlit eyes. "Ditto," she whispered back before adding shyly, "But you must do this all the time... What with all those women screaming at you during your show each night." She hoped she didn't sound jealous.

He laughed dryly. "No. I rarely even give out my real name, let alone date any of them."

She was as surprised as she was thrilled. "Really? Even with all those pretty girls coming up to you after the show?"

"They don't want me. They want Elvis. They don't even know me." He threaded his fingers through hers, staring into her eyes with tender satisfaction. "Come see my band tomorrow night. We're competing in Battle of the Bands. If you're there, I'll sing that much better."

She leaned up on an elbow and looked at him in astonishment. "Band?"

"Yeah, I thought I told you. The Elvis gig is just my day job, so to speak. My real band is playing tomorrow night. Can you come?"

She kissed him, her man of surprises. "Wouldn't miss it for the world."

She still didn't know what could really come of this, she reflected as they got dressed. It was crazy to be so enamored of someone she had met only hours earlier. Yet everything from the dreamy look in his eyes to the searing touch of his fingers told her that they were experiencing something rare and special. T.J. was way too gorgeous and wanted by far too many women for her to even consider losing her heart to him. But as he pulled her into his arms again for a deep and wordless embrace, she suspected she might not have a choice.

Chapter Four

The next day a summer thunderstorm crackled and boomed outside the bookstore where she worked. A typical Saturday, she was kept busy all through her shift, first on the registers and then at the information desk, helping customers find the books they needed. At last her coworker and best friend Leigh arrived after lunch. Vanessa tugged her into the New Age section for a private chat.

"You're not going to believe what happened to me last night," Vanessa whispered. "I met the hottest guy, Leigh—and I am so completely sprung on him."

Leigh pretended to faint. "Hold on a second. Are you telling me that the Summer of Celibacy has ended?"

"Has it ever." A smile of satisfied bliss unfurled across her face.

Her best friend gaped at her. "Tell me everything *now.*"

Keeping an eye out for their supervisor, Vanessa quickly told her friend the entire story—waking up and remembering it was the anniversary of Elvis's death, then meeting one impersonator in the cemetery who led her to T.J. "He's gorgeous and sweet and great in bed and—"

A shy cough silenced her. Both of them turned to see another coworker peeping around a bookcase at them.

"Hi, Vanessa," Gabe said shyly.

Leigh walked off but Vanessa struggled to be polite. "Oh, hi, Gabe."

Gabe was the official bookstore conspiracy nut. At any opportunity, he would discourse on government plots, secret societies and bizarre cults. He had spent the last company Christmas party describing the true mystical meaning of the floating eye and pyramid on the American one dollar bill. Whenever customers came in seeking a book on alien kidnappings or political conspiracies, everyone sent them to Gabe.

Despite his oddball theories, Vanessa knew he was highly intelligent and painfully timid—so she always tried to be nice to him.

He came closer now, his eyes gleaming behind his spectacles. "Did I hear you talking about Elvis's death? Or rather—his alleged death," he added craftily.

She wasn't especially pleased that he had eavesdropped on her conversation. "Gabe, please. You're not referring to those tabloid sightings, are you? Elvis is dead. No one could have pulled off a stunt like that."

"You'd be surprised," Gabe told her with a sinister look. "There are many unresolved questions about his death. *20/20* even did a special on it. Many people believe that it was a wax dummy in the coffin—"

Vanessa glanced around, hoping no one could overhear their conversation. "Gabe, come on."

"I know it sounds crazy. But if you do the research, the evidence all points to Elvis hoaxing his own death. Have you seen the photo of him in his coffin?"

"No, gross! That's so morbid."

"Vanessa—it's not him. The nose is wrong, and the face is much thinner and younger than he'd looked in years. And the coffin weighed nine hundred pounds, despite the fact that both he and the coffin together could only account for about six hundred. A lot of people say there was an air-conditioning unit in the coffin so the wax dummy wouldn't melt."

Oh God, Gabe was crazier than she'd ever realized. "Um, okay," she said. "That's very interesting but—"

"And his life insurance policy was never cashed. We're talking over a million dollars unclaimed all these years. Makes you think someone was afraid to commit insurance fraud, doesn't it?"

"Gabe—look." She was beginning to feel embarrassed. "I just said that guy sounded like him—that's it. He wasn't old enough to be the real Elvis. He was sixty at the most."

"Plastic surgery." Gabe shrugged. "He could afford it. Hey, I agree, it was probably just another impersonator. But you wouldn't be the first person to report meeting Elvis long after his 'death'. Hundreds of people report seeing him every year."

"I have to get back to work." Vanessa hurried back to the information desk. She didn't want to hurt his feelings, but today she wanted to enjoy her lingering physical elation from last night—not get tied up in a weird discussion of faked deaths and oddball conspiracies.

ഇരുതു

An electric tingle still lingered in the air when Vanessa walked out of her house that night in stiletto heels, a short black slip dress and only a tiny scrap of black silk between her legs. The thunderstorm had cooled off the heat, leaving a moist breeze that danced along her bare arms and lifted her short hemline up her thighs. It was the kind of summer night meant for red-hot sex—and after last night's romp with T.J., every cell in her body was crying for it. Yet at the same time, she couldn't deceive herself that this was a matter of simple lust. All day she had been anticipating their date with a euphoric longing that was way too intense for a summer fling. Because that was what this was, right? Regardless of her besotted feelings last night, she had to keep that in mind. Otherwise T.J. would hurt her just like Landon had.

The club hosting the Battle of the Bands was downtown. She'd been there before with Landon to see some of his favorite bands perform but she hadn't gone back since they broke up. A nervous tremor ran through her as she showed her ID at the door. Would he be here tonight?

The club was just as she remembered—a dark sweltering cave of noise and colored lights. Broken glass and cigarette butts crunched beneath her heels as she peered at the band on stage. No, it wasn't T.J.'s band and that was a good thing—they sounded terrible. At the bar she ordered a Diet Coke and Bacardi. She had just paid the bartender when a new song burst out from the stage, and turning, she saw T.J.

He was center stage, flanked by a bassist, guitarist and drummer, but that was the only similarity to his performance last night. Tonight he looked every inch the young rock star, his taut shirtless torso bathed in sweat and his pale eyes glittering with eyeliner. He strutted and shook like a diabolical prince, his black hair artlessly falling around his tanned face as he sang. If she hadn't seen him out of his Elvis persona, she never would have recognized him as the same person.

T.J. was kneeling now, singing with heartfelt passion into the mike. As he tilted his head back, his black hair falling over his tender neck, she realized she liked his band's music. Unlike so much of what her ex-boyfriend listened to, this went beyond

192

earsplitting noise and was actually enjoyable. She sighed with relief.

God, he was so sexy. Every girl in the club was watching him with barely restrained lust, their eyes hot with backstage intentions. But she was the one who had made him moan last night—and she was the one who would be on top of him tonight. A small pang echoed through her pussy at the thought of straddling him later on.

His band finished and left the stage. As the next contender for Battle of the Bands was announced, she headed back to the bar for ice water. The sweltering club had left her throat dry and she didn't want to order a second drink when she was driving.

Someone tapped her hard on the shoulder. She turned to see Landon, her ex-boyfriend, staring at her.

"What are you doing here, Vanessa?" He scanned her short black dress and heels and grew angry. "Jesus, are you even wearing a bra?"

A river of emotions swamped her—shock at seeing him for the first time after three months, pleasure that she was dressed to kill and then annoyance at his tone. "I'm watching my friend's band. Why shouldn't I be here?"

"This isn't your scene, Vanessa. You usually don't even stay out past midnight. What friend and which band?"

She sipped her drink. "The one that just finished. I'm dating the lead singer."

His eyes widened with surprise before swiftly narrowing in jealousy.

"Oh, that's nice," Landon snapped. "You didn't waste any time getting over me, did you?"

Her brows shot up. "Are you serious? We broke up three months ago, Landon. Did you honestly think I spent this whole summer sitting home and pining over you?" There was no reason for him to know that was exactly what she had done— until last night.

"I— You just— You shouldn't be dating a musician, Vanessa. They're wild, they do drugs, they—"

"Act like immature losers? I believe that would be you," she told him, and, taking her drink, vanished into the crowd.

A gleam to her right caught her eye. A familiar face watched her from the wall, the stage lights glinting off his tinted glasses. It was the older Elvis impersonator from the cemetery.

She did a double take, as startled again by his dead-on resemblance to Elvis Presley as she was at seeing him here. Quickly she tried to cut through the crowd to find him. By the time she reached the wall, he was gone.

Weird. The guy had to be a secret fan of T.J.'s. Yet how odd for a sixtyish man to attend the raucous, screaming Battle of the Bands. This was a young crowd.

A hand grabbed her arm and she bristled, ready to tell Landon off. But it was T.J.. His tousled hair was wet with sweat and his grin was triumphant. "Did you hear us?"

She threw her arms around him. "I got here just in time. You were awesome."

He kissed her, the heat of his trembling body burning through her dress. "They won't announce the finalists for a few days. Let's take off."

The high of performing seemed to have ignited T.J.'s libido. In the parking lot he led her between cars, pulling her dress up and tugging her panties down. "I have to have you now," he muttered, his fingers sliding between her legs. She writhed beneath him, caught between fear of exposure and the pleasure of having her pussy so unexpectedly and publicly stimulated. "I saw you from the stage and couldn't wait to get my hands on you..."

"T.J., we're in a parking lot!" She tried to fix her dress but he stopped her.

"So what?" he murmured, his mouth traveling over her cheekbones in an impatient trail of kisses. "No one's watching." He pressed her against the car and slid his leg between hers. "Come on, Vanessa," he whispered, his thigh rubbing her swollen clit. "I can't hold out all the way to my house."

The muscles of his fevered body were shaking against her. Like a contagion, his excitement swept over her. "I don't think I can either." She pushed her hips against him.

"The beach. We'll go there." That fast, he was pulling her through the parking lot to his car.

The wind whipped her long dark hair in her face as T.J. navigated the streets to the beach. Her dress clung to the dampness between her legs as she turned to face him. Naughtily, she kicked her stiletto heel off her left foot and slipped her foot into the crotch of his jeans. His erection felt hard enough to burst. T.J. groaned and looked at her. "Vanessa, don't end this before it gets going..."

In response she only smiled and spread her legs wider. As T.J. frantically tried to keep his eyes on the road, she pulled her black satin panties to the side, exposing all of herself to him. She ran her fingers over the wet pink folds of her pussy, then opened her lips for him. He gripped the steering wheel tightly. "Are you trying to make me have an accident?" he growled.

She had just begun to slide two fingers inside herself when he screeched into the parking lot, killed the engine and dove between her smooth and open legs. The agile strokes of his tongue set a fiery thrill through her body. His fingers replaced

195

the movements of her own, opening up her soft and yielding entrance to fill her pussy with firm, dexterous strokes. His tongue washed over her clit, making her moan, but then he pulled away.

"Beach," he panted.

He led her down across the sand, beyond the jetty where the lights of the parking lot did not reach. Here the waves crashed against the shore with primal force, the sand bathed silver in the moonlight. Vanessa took off her dress and panties and inhaled the oceanic scent of the night, enjoying the cool August breeze across her breasts. She turned to T.J. to find him already naked, his eyes burning with erotic fire. He dropped to his knees and pulled her hips to his face.

She shook her head, tilting her body away from him. "No." He had satisfied her so thoroughly last night. Tonight was his turn. She wanted to sear this night on his memory.

His full lips looked sensual and inviting in the starlight. She traced them with a fingertip, savoring the masculine beauty of the face before her, then knelt opposite him. With avid hunger she took his cock in her hands, squeezing and stroking his hardness until he seemed close to exploding over her fingers. All the while her gaze drank in the tanned, cut pectoral lines of his chest and the abdominal muscles quivering with tension. After seeing him perform his own music on stage tonight, his talent and fire seemed even sexier. She wanted to spend hours exploring his beautiful body.

T.J. seemed to feel differently. "Vanessa, you're teasing me," he said in a choked voice.

She smiled. "Sorry." With one wide stroke of her tongue, she licked off the pre-come glistening on his swollen head. T.J. groaned with appreciation.

Still watching the flush of excitement on his face, Vanessa rubbed his cock over her nipples. Pushing her breasts together around him until his shaft was snug in her cleavage, she began licking his head with broad, firm strokes.

Breathing rapidly, T.J. jerked his hips, trying to drive deep into her mouth. Instead she gripped him tight in the ring of her lips, wiggling her tongue back and forth until his veins pulsed beneath her. His thighs tensed visibly with frustration. To tease him further, she ran her fingernails up and down his muscles until they clenched beneath her touch. She shifted, feeling her own flesh swell and ache. Causing such a gorgeous man to lose control was the ultimate aphrodisiac.

"Vanessa..." T.J.'s voice was tight with demand.

Swallowing a smile, she sucked all of him into her hot mouth, from his head down to his base. T.J. held still for a moment and she knew he was struggling for control. Tantalizingly she ran her tongue down his shaft, then sucked him firmly, drawing out his pleasure with her mouth.

An almost anguished groan escaped him. T.J.'s hips began to pump as her lips and tongue worked him faster. The warm smell of his skin mixed with the salty ocean air, intoxicating her senses. She loved doing this to him, loved making him feel as excited and on fire as she had felt last night. She tongued the sensitive tip of his head, tapping it until he writhed against her. With a final succulent swirl of her tongue, he exploded into her mouth, drenching her with his juices.

He collapsed on the sand, eyes closed in obvious satisfaction. "Oh God... Vanessa..."

She smiled, tracing his perfect lips once more. The salty-sweet taste of him had only made her own throbbing need more urgent. She leaned over him, kissing his hard stomach, and then placed his hand on the soft mound between her legs.

197

Slowly his index finger traced patterns through her curls, grazing her clit to slip down over her tender, aching folds.

She straddled his hand, enjoying the exquisite feel of his cool fingers on her burning flesh. Stretched out on the beach beneath her, T.J. looked like a sleeping god of the moon, impossibly handsome. She dropped to all fours, the sand damp beneath her hands and knees, and lightly began to brush her stiff nipples over his face.

T.J. opened his eyes. The moonlight filled them with a delirious gleam. "You look so fucking sexy," he murmured then sucked her nipple inside the hot soft cushion of his lips.

That familiar fire ignited in her body. A long, deep sigh escaped her as she arched her back, shamelessly pressing herself into his mouth. Part of her had been afraid that last night's magic would never be replicated. Yet the sensation of his tongue circling her breast evoked that same glorious fever filling her veins.

T.J.'s fingers slid deep into her slickness, stroking her inner tunnel in knowledgeable circles that made her gasp. Her own juices were pooling around his hand, and the roar of the surf and the damp sand clinging to her naked body made her feel as primal as an animal. But as she rocked herself toward fulfillment on his expert fingertips, she knew she needed more. She wanted to feel all of him inside her, she wanted to experience the full power and potential of the chemistry between them.

She reached for his cock and palmed the head, coaxing and teasing him back to full hardness. T.J. groaned under her ministrations and reached for a condom. Leaning over, she bit his lower lip before capturing his mouth in a deep, burning kiss. "Fuck me," she whispered into his mouth and turned around, presenting him with the temptation of her behind.

With swift urgency, T.J. reared up on his knees behind her and placed his resuscitated erection against her swollen, soft flesh. With one firm push of his hips, he buried his shaft in her slick heat until his balls rested against her.

Vanessa gave a short gasp that was part lust and part gratitude. Her blood pounded from the excitement of being so completely filled, her walls stretched tight around him. His cock felt magnificently huge within her. For a moment T.J. didn't move as both of them adjusted to the intense desire coursing through them. Slowly he withdrew from her, teasing them both with momentary deprivation before driving back into her depths.

Vanessa's fingernails dug into the sand. "Don't stop," she begged hoarsely. If he stopped, she was sure she would explode. Her body was shaking with the force of her desire and even the slap of his balls against her skin was driving her fever higher and higher. T.J.'s cock was spearing in and out of her, building up in speed and intensity until he was pounding at her in a forceful, relentless rhythm. She closed her eyes and moaned, her breath coming raggedly in time with his thrusts as he fucked her. A white-hot friction was rising in her pussy and it filled her flesh with an almost unbearable tension.

T.J. was grunting urgent, unintelligible things. Leaning over her back, he cupped the fullness of her breasts in his hands and twisted her nipples between his fingers. Vanessa dropped her head and screamed as an orgasm of shattering euphoria ripped through her. The stabbing thrusts of his cock dissolved her nerves into soft, wet heat as she came, her pussy milking him tightly. T.J. squeezed her breasts and held her against him, and with a final thrust, erupted inside her.

Vanessa collapsed on the sand, her legs and arms shaking too hard to hold herself up any longer. Her heart was pounding and she was breathing hard, but a strange sense of exaltation spread through her. T.J. had unlocked feelings inside her that she hadn't known existed, a union of complete emotional and sensual gratification. She reached for his hand as a deep, drowsy contentment stole over her mind, and closed her eyes.

T.J. gathered her into his strong arms, kissing her neck. "You okay?" he whispered. "Vanessa..."

"...Vanessa. Wake up."

She opened her eyes with a scowl, wanting to enjoy this bliss saturating her entire body. The crimson glow of the sun rising over the water jolted her into a sitting position. She had slept in his arms for hours.

T.J. laughed tenderly, brushing the sand from her hair. "You're beautiful when you sleep."

She buried her head in his shoulder, reveling in the contrast between his warm skin and the cool fresh air of daybreak. "Have you been awake this entire time?" She realized with a flash of guilt that he had covered her with his clothes to keep her warm, while he had remained naked.

"Most of it. I was making up song lyrics while I watched you sleep." He kissed her lips.

She groaned. "T.J., you should have woken me up. That must have been so boring for you."

He smoothed her hair back, meeting her gaze with a look of affection that was as enamored as it was serious. "Vanessa, there is nothing boring about being with you. Pretty much every moment we spend together is awesome."

She smiled shakily, not sure of how to respond. The ardent look in T.J.'s eyes told her that he meant his words. But she was afraid to make a fool of herself by telling him just how enthralled she felt in return. She still didn't know if this was just a typical summer fling for him or if this was as rare and special for him as it was for her.

200

"Come on," he said, helping her to her feet. "We should go before the cops kick us out for public indecency."

Still sleepy, she pulled on her dress and panties and walked hand in hand with him back to his car.

Chapter Five

The next afternoon found her at the bookstore's information desk, dreamily watching more warm summer rain drench the parking lot.

"Slow today," Leigh said as she wandered over from the empty cash registers. "When do you get off?"

"Not till closing." T.J. had rehearsal tonight so they wouldn't be seeing each other. He had invited her to come watch after she finished at the store, but she thought a night apart might help her clarify her thoughts. This physical infatuation swimming in her veins was so intense she could think of little else. All day she had been in an erotic fog, tuning out the customers asking her for help. It was as if T.J. had infected her with his own particular brand of sexual magic.

"Vanessa," Leigh said loudly.

"What?"

"I just asked what you were doing tonight. Why are you so spacey today?"

"My hormones," Vanessa muttered. "This guy has put a spell on me."

The truth was that he had cast his spell on her heart as well as her body. She just didn't want to admit that to Leigh or herself. As her attachment to him deepened every day, she felt more and more vulnerable to the kind of emotional devastation that Landon had inflicted upon her—and despite the brevity of their relationship, she sensed that with T.J. that kind of disappointment could hurt just as badly. Somehow she had always known in the back of her mind that she and Landon would self-destruct as a couple. They hadn't had the compatibility to build a life together. Yet when she looked in T.J.'s crystalline eyes or felt his arms go around her, she felt he had the potential to fulfill all of her dreams for the future.

She momentarily toyed with the idea of ending things now, before she fell any harder for him. No, she couldn't. Giving up such a passionate, sensitive man to protect herself was crazy.

Leigh peered closely at her with a frown. "Why are you so preoccupied with him anyhow? He's just a guy."

"He's not just a guy, Leigh. He's...different." Vanessa fiddled with a pad of Post-It notes to avoid her friend's gaze.

"Vanessa, come on. He's supposed to be your rebound fling to help get over Landon. You can't get serious about him. I mean...he's a musician and you know what they're like with women."

Something inside her recoiled at hearing her insecurities articulated so bluntly. "Not all musicians are like that."

"Most of them are," Leigh said cynically. "Look at your beloved Elvis Presley. He cheated on Priscilla left and right."

"T.J. isn't Elvis," Vanessa snapped. "You've never even met him."

"Fine, whatever. I'm just saying you might want to try keeping your mind on work right now —you've got a customer." Leigh vanished back to the registers, where a line was forming, as Vanessa straightened up with a forced cheerful smile.

Her smile dropped as she got a good look at the portly gray-haired man approaching her. It was Elvis—or rather, the

203

middle-aged impersonator from the cemetery. Just like the other day, he wore a baseball cap. At first glance, he looked like anyone else.

"Oh my God—hi." Surprise at seeing him in her store left her tongue-tied.

"Not God, just the King," he kidded with a broad smile. "You got time to help out an old man?"

At the sound of that beloved familiar voice, a nostalgic warmth filled her whole body. She knew it was silly but she couldn't help but feel honored, as if Elvis himself really had chosen to visit her.

"Of course," she said shyly.

Despite the rain, he was still wearing his big tinted glasses. The blue eyes behind them were reassuringly kind. "Your boyfriend did a good job last night."

"Yes, he did." A million questions raced through her mind. "So why did you send me to the show the other night when you weren't there? I thought you were the impersonator but instead I met T.J..."

He winked at her. "You saying you'd have it the other way around?"

"Well, yes—I mean, no, because of T.J. but—well, listen, I want to see you perform. Just hearing you talk gives me the shivers. Hearing you sing must be incredible."

That broad smile spread over his face. Somehow it strengthened the resemblance even more. A funny pang went off in her stomach and she looked closer at him.

"I need a book," he said. "Can you help me with that?"

"Oh...sure." Here she was as flustered as her mom would have been around the real Elvis. She resolved to be more composed as she slipped out from behind the information desk. "What was it?"

To her surprise, he was looking for a book on numerology. She led him over to the New Age section, grateful that conspiracy theorist Gabe wasn't on shift, and they looked through the available titles. He didn't seem interested in any of them. "The book is called *Cheiro's Book of Numbers*. Can you order it?"

"Oh sure." She led him back to the information desk, where she looked up the ISBN of the book and discovered it was an old book, not kept in stock. "Not that that means anything," she told him. "We can easily order you a copy. How'd you hear of this book?"

"It's an old favorite of mine."

"It shouldn't take long to come in..." Her voice trailed off when she noticed a large ring on his hand. It consisted of the initials TCB. She realized those were probably his initials and remembered that she didn't know his name. She raised her head, feeling foolish again. "By the way, I'm Vanessa."

He extended a hand and they shook, but he did not volunteer his own name.

"And you are?" she prompted.

He tilted his head, smiling that famous smile. Then he said, "You can call me Jon."

"Okay." Somehow it was disappointing to associate such an everyday name with him. *Oh be real, Vanessa,* she scolded herself. *Like he really wanted you to call him Elvis.*

She searched for a pen and paper. "If you just write down your name and phone number, we'll call you as soon as your copy arrives. There's no commitment—you can look at it first and decide if you still want it."

He only pushed the pen and paper back at her with that inscrutable smile.

"Uh... Did you change your mind?" she asked, puzzled.

"That's not going to work. I'll just come back."

She stared at him. His blue eyes stared back at hers through the tinted lenses in a challenge...a challenge to know who he really was. That strange excited flutter began in her stomach again and her skin rose up in tiny goose bumps as she took in the whole of his face once more—the curve of his lips, his bedroom eyes, even his distinctive nose. It was all so familiar, yet looked so strange framed by that gray hair and his casual clothes.

"I'll be seeing you," he said with a smile and walked out of the bookstore.

Every cell in her body wanted to leap over the desk and go after him as she watched him leave. *That's Elvis Presley. That is really, truly Elvis Presley as an old man. I know it is.*

Leigh wandered back over. "Who was that guy? He looked familiar."

"That...that was the Elvis impersonator I told you about."

Leigh's eyes bugged out in astonishment. "That's your sexy new boyfriend? That old guy?"

"No. He's the guy I met in the cemetery."

"Oh. How can he impersonate Elvis with gray hair?" Leigh checked her cell phone, then slid it back in her pocket. "Listen, let's get a drink after work."

"I can't, Leigh. I've got something I have to do."

As soon as Leigh left, she looked up Gabe's number and called him. This mystery man was driving her crazy, and she needed to know facts that only Gabe could teach her.

৪০৪০৪০

A rainbow-like aura circled the August moon as she hesitated in Gabe's driveway that night. He had invited some conspiracy buff friends over to "explain" the facts of Elvis's death to her but now she was paralyzed by feelings of foolishness and curiosity. What was she doing?

Gabe popped his head out the front door. "Come on in," he said cheerfully. "We're dying to hear all about this guy."

To her relief, the three guys awaiting her inside looked normal—that is normal considering they spent their spare time creating websites dedicated to Bigfoot, aliens and suspicious celebrity deaths. After offering her a drink, Gabe sat her down at the kitchen table and paused over his notebook. "Before your mind is influenced by what we show you, I want to transcribe your notes. Tell us everything that happened, Vanessa—what this guy said, what he wore, how he looked."

Taking a deep breath, she complied. But as she described his sweatshirt, gray sideburns and casual demeanor, she realized how absurd it all sounded. This guy hadn't said or done anything to indicate he was Elvis Presley. It was just the dead-on resemblance, and she had no way to show them that, did she?

"And you didn't get a name, right?" Gabe asked, writing furiously.

"Today, I did. But all he said was 'Jon'. He might as well have said John Smith."

She was surprised by the excited look the other guys exchanged. "I don't think it was his real name," she added. "He was wearing this big ring with initials on it and there wasn't a J—"

All four men went absolutely still. "What initials?" one asked in a hushed voice.

She stared at them. "TCB."

All of them exploded into shouts of satisfaction and excitement. "It's him," one shouted. "It's got to be."

Vanessa held up a hand for calm. "Can you please explain what's such a big deal? Elvis's initials were EAP—Elvis Aron Presley."

"TCB stands for *Taking Care of Business*," they told her jubilantly. "It's carved on his gravestone and he had a custom-made ring with those initials."

She absorbed this information. "Well, a thorough impersonator might get one made himself."

"Elvis also used an alias for his drug-enforcement work— Jon Burrows," Gabe informed her. "Supposedly he's been spotted quite a bit up in Kalamazoo, Michigan, at a building owned by a Jon Burrows."

"Hold on," she said. "Drug enforcement?"

A happy smile rippled over Gabe's face. "Oh, Vanessa, do we have a lot to tell you."

For the next three hours Vanessa underwent a crash course on the final years—and after—of Elvis Presley.

First they showed her photos of his gravestone, featuring a misspelled middle name.

Then they showed her an unexplained photo of Elvis taken through the screen door of his pool house—but taken four months after his death. Gabe showed her a photo of Elvis taken right before his death, heavyset and tired-looking, and contrasted it with a photo of his corpse in his coffin, looking oddly young and slim with a strange pug nose. "Not the same person," he said. "Furthermore, people reported the body as sweating—which dead bodies don't do—and as looking fake, like wax."

Wax corpses? Misspelled tombstones? She was beginning to feel like an idiot.

"Elvis was supposed to start a tour the day he died," one of his friends told her. "Yet he failed to order a single new jumpsuit, despite the fact he'd gained too much weight to fit into his old ones. People also found it odd that they were able to autopsy the body, return it to the house, order a special coffin, arrange a very extensive funeral and have thousands of T-shirts and new albums printed—all in less than a day."

Her head was beginning to hurt. Yes, it all sounded very suspicious. But it was still hard to believe. "I don't understand the drug-enforcement part," she said.

"Elvis met with President Nixon and became a drug-enforcement agent," Gabe explained. "That's a documented fact. Some people theorize that as a result of his undercover work, he ran afoul of someone shady and was having his life threatened. Maybe the best way to protect his family was to fake his own death."

"He had the government connections to pull it off," a friend added.

"But..." Vanessa was bothered by too many unanswered questions. "He'd be an old man by now. In his seventies. This guy was sixty at the most... And why would he just be walking around in public?"

"You didn't recognize him at first," Gabe pointed out. "Having gray hair and wearing sunglasses is probably all the disguise he needs. As for looking young, so do a lot of celebrities that age. Elvis could certainly afford the surgery."

One of his friends leaned forward. "Vanessa, we're not saying it's him. We're just saying there are a lot of good reasons to think Elvis Presley did not die in 1977."

She rubbed her eyes. It was almost one a.m. and she had absorbed all of the Internet sites and conspiracy theories she could. "I don't know. I believe that he could have hoaxed his death. But I don't believe it could be kept quiet all these years. Sooner or later, someone would have talked. The temptation to make a fortune off such a hot story would be too great."

"You're forgetting that they would need proof," Gabe said gently. "You've seen this guy twice, but so what? If you called a journalist right now, you'd be a laughingstock."

That was true. She stood. "It's late." She had a lot to think about, and she was beginning to wish she'd just gone to T.J.'s rehearsal. "Thanks for showing me all of this."

Gabe had a zealous gleam in his eye. "Vanessa, if he ever comes into the store when I'm there..."

"I'll tell you for sure." She patted his shoulder as she walked out. "Thanks, guys."

Driving home, she couldn't stop thinking about everything she had learned. Would she see "Jon" again? If so, what should she say? "Hi, I think you're Elvis Presley. By the way, why exactly have you been hanging around so much?" It was all so crazy...and yet she couldn't shake the conviction deep in her bones that it was really, truly him.

Chapter Six

The next night T.J. took her to the carnival. For two hours they slammed together on the Tilt-A-Whirl, screamed on the roller coaster and shrieked and laughed in the haunted house. On the Ferris wheel they kissed so urgently at the top that Vanessa didn't realize they had descended until the ride master pointedly cleared his throat. The revolving colored lights, merry electronic tunes and games played over her senses in a dizzying elation until she hugged T.J.'s waist for support.

Although he occasionally spotted revue regulars walking around the carnival, none of them recognized him as their favorite Elvis impersonator, which she found amusing.

He kissed her hair. "Hungry?"

"Starving."

They bought baskets of fried shrimp with big wax cups of soda and ice and ate it on the beach. The greasy food tasted better to Vanessa than any meal this summer. The sand was soft under her bare toes and the briny scent of the ocean made her feel achingly alive. Maybe it was already mid-August, but these last few nights with T.J. had given her the summer romance of her dreams. She cast a longing glance at him. He looked so handsome tonight in faded jeans and a black T-shirt, the sea breeze ruffling his black hair.

Unbidden, yesterday's argument with Leigh surfaced in her mind. *He's a musician and you know what they're like with women.* It reminded her that summer was almost over. The Celebrity Star Revue would end when the carnival did after Labor Day. Would T.J. consign her to the rest of his summer memories and start a new chapter in his life? She brought their shrimp containers to a wastebasket on the sand, letting seagulls pick at the remains of their dinner. As she walked back, she tried to think of a way to bring up his future plans.

"So why aren't you performing tonight?" she asked when she returned.

"There's a regular concert scheduled tonight." He shot a rock into the water. "I'll be glad when summer's over and this gig ends with it. I need to focus on my band."

"Will you be Elvis next summer?"

"Depends on how successful the band is. The revue money's good but it eats up too much of my time." He began to idly draw in the sand three letters: TCB. "As Elvis himself would say, you gotta take care of business. And my priority is my career...not imitating someone else's."

Her stomach clenched. All night she had been thinking of a way to discuss yesterday's findings with him and now he had given her the perfect opportunity.

"Um...right. Speaking of which, guess who came to see me at the bookstore yesterday?"

T.J. gave her a suspicious sidelong glance that reminded her intensely of a young Elvis. "Who?"

"The other impersonator. The one I met at the cemetery." She wanted desperately to deliver all of this in a casual, plausible manner but her throat was dry with nervousness. "He kind of spooked me, T.J. I mean...he looks exactly like Elvis. Exactly."

She waited for him to respond. Instead he shot another rock into the water. When he spoke, his voice was flat. "So?"

"So... It sounds crazy, but what if? I was talking to these guys last night who research this stuff and they provided me with a lot of compelling evidence that Elvis Presley didn't die in 1977. It's really astonishing when you look at the photos and analyze the lack of documentation and compare the conflicting stories and—"

"Vanessa, Elvis is dead. He was abusing prescription drugs and he was in bad health and he keeled over on the toilet and died. It's that simple." His body shifted away from her.

"I know that's probably what happened. But if you could have seen this guy. His eyes, his lips... And he was wearing the same TCB ring as Elvis and he asked for a book that turned out to be Elvis's favorite book—"

T.J. moved away so that he was facing her. His blue eyes shone with incredulity in the night. "How naive are you? You're twenty-six and gorgeous. Some old fart comes on to you in the cemetery and drops hints that he's Elvis and you totally buy into it. This guy is just playing you, don't you get that?"

"It wasn't like that." Her face grew flushed with annoyance. "For one thing, he's the one who steered me to you. Secondly—"

"He suggested you go to the show doubtless so he could meet you there. He was probably in the audience, waiting to buy you a drink until he saw me kiss you."

She shook her head. "You haven't even met this guy. He's really sweet."

"Vanessa, give me a break. Did you tell him where you worked? If not, how did he know? Sounds like a stalker to me." T.J. scoffed as he got to his feet. "I can't believe this. I thought you were different."

She stood, her blood going hot with indignation. "What's that supposed to mean?"

"It means that I thought you liked me for me. That's why I told you I worked the lights crew, because I wanted to see if you'd still want me. But it turns out you're just another Elvis groupie."

"I am not!" she said, deeply stung. "How dare you?"

"How dare I?" His eyes were like ice. "You've got to be kidding. Ever since I put on sideburns and a jumpsuit, I've had women of all ages trying to get in my pants, calling me Elvis and begging me to talk like him. They want to sleep with *him*—not me. And you're just the same. Hell, you're worse—one of those loony tunes who believes he's alive."

"I am not loony tunes." An incandescent fury was spreading through her body. "I am trying to have a reasonable discussion with you based on logic and evidence, and you've totally flipped out. If anyone's loony tunes, it's you."

"Oh, yeah, right. Listen, when I go on stage and sing 'Hound Dog', I know it's an act. But you think it's the real thing." His tanned face was tight with betrayal. "Go sleep with your old middle-aged Elvis, Vanessa. Apparently you think he's closer to the real thing than I am."

"What?" she exclaimed. "I don't want to sleep with him. I want you. I want—"

T.J. turned his back on her and strode away across the beach.

"T.J.!" she cried after him. Panic and despair spread through her body in a cold wave. "Don't do this!"

He only walked off into the night without answering. She stared after him, the ocean breeze whipping her hair across her eyes as they filled with tears.

ജ്ഞ

Vanessa was listless and quiet at the bookstore the next day. Her throat ached with fresh unshed tears and her mind replayed her argument with T.J. on a loop. It seemed impossible that such a promising relationship could end over a ridiculous fight about an Elvis impersonator. Surely she could resolve the misunderstanding between them. Yet then she would wonder if T.J. even wanted it resolved. Maybe she really had been just a summer fling to him and this was his way of terminating it before it went stale.

All day she battled the impulse to call him. The store was busy with back-to-school shoppers and she was grateful to be placed at the registers, where neither Leigh nor Gabe could approach her. She dreaded telling Leigh that her hot summer romance was already over and she knew Gabe was eager to discuss her Elvis "sighting". She was sorry now that she had told him about it, sorry she had ever met Elvis or "Jon" or whoever he was.

All the same, she kept an anxious eye on the doors, hoping "Jon" would come back. But he did not return—and T.J. did not call to apologize.

At last her shift was over. She slipped out before Leigh or Gabe could stop her and headed straight for the cemetery. Somehow she needed to speak to her mother—or at least return to her grave where this had all started.

It was another peaceful summer twilight, just like last week. She crouched down in front of her mother's tombstone and stared at the carved numbers spelling out her mother's birth and death. It wasn't fair that her mother had died so young of breast cancer; it also wasn't fair that the world had lost one of its greatest stars at forty-two. But her mother was definitely gone and Elvis probably was too.

"Hey, darlin'."

She turned to see him behind her. "Jon", looking as casual as ever in jeans and baseball cap. His sunglasses were tucked into the neck of his shirt and the effect of his pale blue eyes was intensified in the dusk. She wiped her eyes and stood up.

"You know, I thought you were bringing me good luck at first," she said. "But now I think it's more like you ruined my summer." She knew it was a childish thing to say but she couldn't help but resent him for her fight with T.J.

The man absorbed this thoughtfully. "I guess summer wasn't always such a lucky time for me either. Checking out in August the way I did."

Her mouth fell open.

"Got married in the spring. Had my daughter in the winter. Yeah, I guess summer wasn't really my season."

Her lips were shaking. She couldn't be hearing this. Everything T.J. had said last night about "Jon" being a crazy old stalker made more sense than this. And yet the somber expression in his blue eyes told her it was the truth. "Are you... Are you trying to tell me that it's really you? Oh my God."

Elvis gave her a look of sad and infinite patience.

"Oh wow. Oh wow." She put her hands in her hair, trying to think. She was speaking to Elvis Presley. The real Elvis Presley. The rumors were true—he had faked his death. She had just uncovered the biggest celebrity mystery ever.

"But..." She couldn't think clearly. "I mean, why tell me? How do you know I won't go tell the whole world, sell my story to the media?"

"I suppose you could do that," he said mildly.

"But no one would believe me, right?" Her eyes ran over him in wild exuberance, memorizing everything—his belly, his scuffed tennis shoes, his gray hair. Trying to be stealthy, her left hand reached for her cell phone and slyly activated the camera function.

"Some would, some wouldn't." He still seemed calm and unafraid of what she might do.

With shaking hands, Vanessa raised her phone and took his picture. To her surprise, he did not even flinch. She was flushed with victory and excitement. "I know to everyone else this will just be a photo of a guy in sunglasses and a baseball cap," she began, looking down to check the photo. "But at least to me—" She stared at the screen. Nothing was on the picture but trees and graves.

She looked up and gasped. Elvis Presley in all his youthful magnificence stood before her—rich black hair and sideburns, narrow-hipped with those deadly blue eyes. He smiled at her.

"You really did die," she said softly.

"Well, now maybe I did and maybe I didn't. What is dying, Vanessa? My poor abused body giving out on the throne?" He grinned to show he considered dying on the toilet a joke. "My memory lives on in the hearts of millions who swear they see me in Hawaii and at Graceland and all over the world. So maybe in some ways I am still alive."

She tried to force her lips into a smile, but they were shaking. "I don't want you to go." Somehow she knew she would never see him again.

"But I have to, darlin'. We all have to eventually." He cocked his head and regarded her through those blue eyes that still shone brightly.

To her surprise, she began to weep. Tears of gratitude blurred her vision and flowed down her cheeks as she grasped

217

the miracle of what had happened to her in the last week. She really had met Elvis Presley—and she really had found love. "Don't go."

He put a hand to her cheek, though she felt only a prickling energy. "Don't cry," he said kindly. "Your summer may get lucky yet." He turned and walked away. When she wiped her eyes and looked up, the cemetery was empty.

Chapter Seven

An hour later Vanessa was running through the carnival, heart pumping with the desperate urge to find and speak with T.J. before he went onstage. She knew now beyond a shadow of a doubt that what they had was meaningful and real, and she had to fix things between them before it was too late. The swirling lights of the Tilt-A-Whirl and Ferris wheel played over her face, giving the night the feeling of a monstrous dream. At last she reached the auditorium and headed straight for the stage doors around back. As she headed down the corridor to the dressing rooms, she could hear shouting.

"Godammit, T.J., I've been more than fair," the stage manager barked. "But this other band of yours is ruining our show."

"This other band is my career!" T.J. snapped back. He was dressed in jeans and a T-shirt, not his Elvis clothes, and his blue eyes were bright with fury. "You know I love performing here, Ben, but I'm not going to be an Elvis impersonator forever. Tonight is the opportunity of a lifetime—I have to take it."

He did a double take as he saw Vanessa. "We made it into the Battle of the Band finals," he told her. "Our band made it into the final three, Vanessa—and we have to go on in two hours. The guys are waiting for me."

He pushed his black jumpsuit at the stage manager. "I'm sorry, Ben. Fire me if you want but I absolutely cannot be Elvis tonight."

Just then the opening chords of "Are you Lonesome Tonight?" drifted backstage.

"Oh Jesus," moaned the stage manager. "They're waiting for you to come out. Look what you've done."

"I'm sorry," T.J. said simply. "I really am. But I have to sing my own music. I think even Elvis would understand that."

Suddenly a haunting voice began to sing the opening words on stage. Vanessa, T.J. and the stage manager all stared at each other before racing for the stage.

Elvis was singing before the crowd. Dressed in a white jumpsuit, thick sunglasses obscuring his eyes, he delivered an unforgettable rendition of the poignant song Vanessa had cried to so many nights this summer.

The crowd burst into thunderous applause as he finished. "Thank you—thank you very much," he said and walked offstage in the opposite direction. The awestruck band looked at each other in astonishment as the emcee rushed after him. Vanessa knew they would find no one.

"Now that's an impersonator," the stage manager breathed. "I've never seen anyone do Elvis like that. How the hell'd you line him up, T.J.?"

"I—uh—" T.J.'s jaw worked helplessly.

"Right, you've got your band gig. Go on, have fun. Forget everything I said—you more than made up for it."

Without a word, T.J. pulled Vanessa into the parking lot and straight to his car. She slid into the passenger seat and he gunned off into the night.

"Vanessa..." He glanced over, his eyes searching hers with remorse. "I was such an ass to you last night. It's just that the whole Elvis thing, well, makes women crazy. I never know if it's me or Elvis they want."

She turned to face him, the wind blowing her long black hair across her face. "I don't want Elvis. I want you."

She realized it was true. The Elvis mystery was just a side trip, a fascinating sexual fantasy of sideburns, swiveling hips and that oh-so-sensual sneer. Her man, the one she wanted to hold forever in her arms, was a star in his own right and there was no one else she'd rather have.

Around two a.m., after T.J.'s band had won the Battle of the Bands and he was photographed by the local paper, T.J. drove her back to collect her car. The carnival was dark and empty, the grounds littered with discarded tickets, spilled popcorn and unwanted prizes. The scent of fried dough and cotton candy still lingered heavily in the air, the roller coaster and merry-go-round ghostly and quiet as they passed. In just two weeks, Vanessa realized again, the carnival would be gone. Summer was almost over. But she knew now that what she and T.J. had would last so much longer.

T.J. seemed to be thinking the same thing as he led her past the parking lot and to the beach. He wrapped the warm strength of his arms around her as together they watched the tide roll in.

"So that man on stage tonight..." T.J.'s voice faded into baffled awe. "Vanessa, it was him, wasn't it?"

She nodded. "Yes. It was him."

"But everyone in the place saw him. They heard him sing. Someone must have tracked him down—"

She shook her head. "They'll never find him, T.J. Trust me."

He looked confused but she would explain later, she decided. Right now, looking up at his brilliant eyes in the moonlight, she wanted only to reconnect with the innate magic between them.

Slowly Vanessa began to undress her favorite singer, removing his T-shirt, jeans and black cotton briefs as if his tight, tanned body was the most anticipated gift she'd ever had the privilege of unwrapping. She ran her hands down his smooth chest and narrow hips, then sought his lips in a kiss that spread a sensation through her body like melting honey. His mouth swept down across her throat, leaving a burning trail on her skin. Vanessa dropped her head back with a moan. The moon was bright and she felt almost drugged as T.J.'s hands lifted her shirt to explore her breasts with torturous slowness.

Vanessa stepped back to admire him. The rhythmic wash of the surf filled her ears as she drank all of him in, from his sculpted face down to his long, muscular legs. From the waist up, T.J. looked as flawless and cut in the moonlight as a statue, only the ocean breeze ruffling his black hair. Yet below the waist his cock was stiffening to an impressive size, its engorged head gleaming with a pearly drop of pre-come in the moonlight. Vanessa ran her fingertips down his stomach, savoring the feel of his taut muscles. As she took his shaft in both of her hands, squeezing and rubbing him until he pulsated in her hands like living marble, a warm arousal unfurled inside her.

T.J. let out a primitive growl, pawing roughly at her bra and shorts until her clothes tumbled to the sand. Now they were both naked and the proximity of his swollen cock only inches from her pussy excited her. He rolled her stiff nipples between his fingers, gently pulling them out from her body until she arched her back, desperate for more.

The ache between her legs was reaching fever pitch. She knelt on the cool, damp sand, her thighs already wet with excitement, as he retrieved a condom from his pocket and knelt opposite her. With trembling fingers she spread her knees and guided him inside her.

His cock felt like heaven. She bit her lip with joy, his hot thrusts sending an electric current up her spine. Together they coupled in a fast and perfect rhythm, their stomachs slapping as he drove in and out of her wet, tight suction. A euphoric fire spread through her body as his gaze burned into hers with a relentless passion that told her he felt just as intensely as she did. On and on he speared in and out of her until their skin was gleaming with sweat.

Panting, Vanessa slid her fingers down her navel, forming a tight V around his thrusts. The resulting friction unleashed a hot bolt of excitement inside her that seemed to reach from her nipples down to her toes. She closed her eyes, her breasts slapping wildly against his pecs, as she felt her slickness pool around his cock.

Rocking faster, T.J. pulled her close and drove deep into her core with an urgent, primal groan. Immediately her pussy dissolved into blissful contractions, milking T.J.'s shaft as he exploded inside her.

Both of them collapsed exhausted and wet on the sand. When he caught his breath, T.J. gathered her into his arms. He turned her chin to look into her eyes.

"This was such a boring summer until I met you," he said, kissing her softly. "But in less than a week you've made it the best summer of my life."

She kissed him back, slow and sweet. "But summer's almost over now…"

"Then I guess you'll be making it the best year of my life." He leaned in to kiss her again when a shooting star rocketed across the August sky.

"Make a wish," T.J. told her.

As she made her silent wish, a song began to play. From somewhere across the ocean, or perhaps from the empty carnival, the distant refrains of an Elvis song drifted toward them. They looked at each other.

"Appropriate song," T.J. said, his arms tightening around her. "Because you know what? I really can't help falling in love with you."

Secure in his arms, Vanessa looked into the night sky and gave a silent thanks to that very real star who had made her wish come true.

About the Author

Veronica Wilde is a passionate book addict whose work has spanned multiple genres. Copywriting is her day job but her true love is fiction, particularly anything involving the paranormal. A former New Yorker, currently she lives in Arizona with her boyfriend and the three cats who own them.

To learn more about Veronica, please visit www.veronicawilde.com. Send an email to Veronica at veronicawilde@yahoo.com.

Her family, her friends and her conscience all say it's wrong to fall for the hustler she rescued from the streets. How come it feels so right?

Finding Home
© 2006 Bonnie Dee and Lauren Baker

Her family, her friends and her conscience all say it's wrong to fall for the hustler she rescued from the streets. How come it feels so right?

When Megan first meets Mouth, a homeless teenage hustler, on the streets of L.A., he's the perfect subject for the street life expose she hopes will help her break into journalism. She doesn't expect to be drawn into his life and become his friend—or to take him in after he's been beaten and robbed by thugs.

As they learn to live together, a powerful attraction flourishes between Megan and the young man. Although he's street smart, tough and mature, he's also a youth in transition. When they finally give in to the sexual heat between them, Megan fears she's taking advantage of her position as his mentor.

Their relationship challenges every aspect of her life. Megan must make difficult choices between the conflicting demands of her friends and family, her career and love.

Available now in ebook and print from Samhain Publishing.

Enjoy the following excerpt from Finding Home…

They were the first to arrive. Stevie greeted them at the door, hugging Megan and shaking Sean's hand before taking the wine from Megan.

Megan watched him closely. Stevie was the only one of the friends present today who hadn't met Sean before finding out about their relationship. He was also thoughtful, rational, a good judge of character, and his opinion would influence the others. So she was a little apprehensive about his reaction.

"What can I get you guys, some beer? A glass of wine? Anything else?"

"You should try Stevie's beer. He's got this real microbrew fetish and always has something new to try out," Megan told Sean. "But beware of the spiel he'll try to feed you about the best brewing methods."

Sean looked at her, the ghost of a smile flitting across his face. "Hey, I'm a guy. I can handle beer talk," he said, mock-serious. The tension eased in her stomach. This was working. The boys could be cool with each other.

"I'll go see how Sasha's doing, then. And Stevie? I'd love a white wine, please. How come James isn't here yet? He never turns down an occasion to raid your beer cellar before eating."

As it turned out, Megan discovered in the kitchen that James and his waitress had just called to warn they'd be late due to car trouble. Allegedly, because as Sasha told her while they took out the pumpkin pie and put it on a plate, he'd sounded very out of breath on the phone. She was prepared to bet whatever had been slowing them down wasn't engine-related.

"You think he called you in mid-fuck?" Megan asked, chuckling.

"I think he was in the car, actually. And I think Ms. Waitress is a pretty limber girl who might just have been giving him a blowjob at that point."

Megan laughed. "Well, at least he's bound to be in a good mood when they arrive."

She was right. When James walked in ten minutes later towing a very pretty, young and remarkably well-endowed blonde behind him, he was in exuberant spirits. "Hey, everybody, meet Kerry!" He kissed Megan and Sasha, hugged Stevie, and nodded briefly at Sean, his expression neutral.

Kerry hugged everyone all around, and kissed Stevie and Sean enthusiastically to their obvious delight.

Megan bit her tongue when she saw Sean's eyes drawn to Kerry's chest for at least ten seconds before he snapped them back up. He caught her looking at him and made a sheepish face.

While everyone milled around the living room, pouring drinks and exchanging greetings, Sean pressed close to Megan and whispered in her hair, "Totally fake. I'll take yours anytime." His hand brushed against her ass in a lascivious caress that sent messages of lust through her body.

They sat down to eat shortly after. Sasha's spread was opulent enough to satisfy the most exacting of standards. Megan thought even her mom would have been impressed. She certainly was. The turkey was impressive, and the table was crammed with mounds of mashed potatoes, candied yams, cornbread, several salads, cranberry sauce and pickles.

Sean pulled up a chair directly across from Megan. James's bimbo sat next to him, flashing him a grin that slightly annoyed Megan. Less so when she felt Sean's foot slyly rubbing her ankle in a gesture designed to evoke both reassurance and desire.

Conversation flowed around the dinner table, fuelled by alcohol, food, and longstanding friendship. Megan noted with pleasure that Sean sometimes joined in, in his reserved way, and his dry humor struck a chord with her friends. She was especially pleased to see Stevie engage him a couple of times and nod approvingly at her when he caught her watching them. James was less friendly, scowling at Sean occasionally, but managed to hold back from making rude comments.

Kerry was the classic ditzy L.A. blonde, complete with aspirations to make it in the movies and a brain roughly as small as her cup size was large. The guys, of course, cut her plenty of slack. But Megan caught James's eye during a particularly inane tirade about cosmetic surgery and he looked embarrassed. She might have teased Kerry a little if Sean's sock-clad foot hadn't been insistently stroking her inner thigh in the most distracting manner.

"You can't be serious!" Sasha's voice rose with indignation. "You think it's right that teenagers should get breast implants? You don't think that's maybe a little premature?"

Sean's foot slid farther up Megan's thigh, inhibiting higher brain functions and preventing her from joining in the debate without her voice betraying her. She looked across at him.

His face was impassive, head tilted slightly to the side, as though listening to the conversation, but Megan knew he was completely focused on her right now. His eyes were the only clue to what was happening under the table, the blue edged out by his dilated pupils.

"Well, you know, Sasha, I had these done when I was nineteen. You can't see the scars. I'll show you in the bathroom if you want. The surgeon who did them was a real pro. My dad paid for them. He said nothing was too good for his princess. And I haven't regretted it yet," Kerry said proudly.

There was a pause as her words sank in. James cringed and poked at his mashed potatoes.

Megan tuned out of the conversation then as Sean's toe reached her underwear and started pressing against her crotch. She focused all her concentration on keeping her breathing even and not making any noise. She wouldn't be able to keep it going for long. He pushed against her clit, harder, and she had to bite back a moan. Kerry might be monopolizing the attention right now, but if Megan had an orgasm at the table, she was pretty sure she'd steal the show.

Sean stared at her, lips slightly parted, and when their eyes locked, he smiled crookedly.

Megan kept her gaze on him as she slowly pushed back her chair to give him a chance to pull his foot away unobtrusively. The loss of contact made her want to cry out, but she couldn't handle the torture anymore. She stood and said in a surprisingly steady voice, "Anyone for coffee?"

In the kitchen, she filled the coffee machine with water and measured out the coffee. A couple of minutes later, Sean appeared in the doorway carrying stacks of plates. He put them on the counter and moved in on her, one arm snaking around her waist, his other hand to the back of her neck. He pulled her in close for a kiss, his mouth hungry on hers and his cock pressing into her crotch. Megan brought her hands up to either side of his face, winding her fingers into his shaggy hair. She moaned softly into his mouth as their tongues entwined, hoping the sound wouldn't carry to the main room.

They kissed urgently for a couple minutes and only pulled apart when Stevie called out to Sean, "Hey man, want to watch some football while the chicks make the coffee and clear the table? Ow! Jesus, Sash, can't you take a joke?"

"You into the football?" Megan whispered.

"Not at the moment." Sean's hand slipped down to her hip and slid under her skirt. His fingers crept up her thigh, following the trail led by his foot earlier.

Megan's every pore reacted to him. She was close to letting him fuck her in the kitchen, not caring who walked in.

"Right now I want to fuck you." His husky voice sent shivers through her body. Her nipples stood erect, pressing against the fabric of her shirt.

Sean's other hand flicked across her chest, sending fire from her sensitive tits straight down to her sex.

She caught her breath. "Go check out the game and meet me in the back bathroom in ten minutes. Through the main bedroom on the left. I'll get the coffee done and after that, I don't give a damn."

He grinned. "Good thing I came prepared, huh?"

Ten minutes later, the coffee was on the table and Megan was in the master bath, hoping neither of their hosts would feel the need to use it in the near future.

She stood in front of the sink, looking at herself in the mirror. Her face was flushed, her eyes dark and bright, and she felt wired and intensely alive. This was crazy. Any of her close friends could walk in on them, but she didn't care, as long as Sean showed up.

GREAT cheap FUN

Discover eBooks!
THE FASTEST WAY TO GET THE HOTTEST NAMES

Get your favorite authors on your favorite reader, long before they're out in print! Ebooks from Samhain go wherever you go, and work with whatever you carry—Palm, PDF, Mobi, and more.

Printed in the United States
112304LV00014B/54/P